SECRET

Also in this series

Look out for...

Secret Simon

Jean Ure

**Hodder
Children's
Books**

a division of Hodder Headline plc

A Catalogue record for this book is available
from the British Library

ISBN 0 340 72724 1

Typeset by Avon Dataset Ltd, Bidford-on-Avon, Warks

Printed and bound in Great Britain by
Clays Ltd, St Ives plc

Hodder Children's Books
a division of Hodder Headline plc
338 Euston Road
London NW1 3BH

1

'Foster by name and foster by nature!'

That was what my dad said when he and Mum decided they were going to apply to be foster parents. It's one of his best jokes. He tells it to everyone! Even sometimes to people who don't realise that our surname is Foster, and then of course they don't get it. I must have heard Dad's joke about a hundred times. But I still laugh, as I wouldn't like to hurt his feelings.

When word came through that we had passed the test – that we were fit for fostering! – Mum and Dad were ever so pleased. I was, too! Before then, I'd thought that I was doomed to be an only child for the rest of my days. Mum was a tiny bit worried that I might find it difficult to share and not be jealous, but I told her I just couldn't wait to have another child in the house! I'd always wanted a sister, for as long as I could remember. I'd never specially wanted a brother. In fact, I'd never really wanted a brother at all. So I just assumed, automatically, that we'd foster a girl.

And we did! 'Cos Sam came to live with us; and me and Sam are almost exactly the same age, we go to the same school and are in the same class, and are just as close as if we were real sisters. Which we practically are, by now!

A short while after Sam came, the lady from Social Services, Miss Davies, asked us if we could take the Radish. Well, *she* didn't call him the Radish, she called him Gus. Me and Sam started calling him Radish on account of his surname being Radice, pronounced Rad–ee–chay. Also because he has bright red hair which grows to a little twizzly point on top of his head!

But the Radish was only six years old when he came to us, so although I all of a sudden found myself with a brother as well as a sister, it was only a very *little* sort of brother. Not like having a great big loutish boy such as Gary Copestake living with us. (Gary Copestake is a boy at school. He and his best friend Charlie Potts used to make our lives a misery – well, my life; not Sam's. Sam just ignored them. She is made of sterner stuff than I am).

You might have thought that having three children in the house was enough for anyone, but one night the Social Services people rang up in a great fluster to ask if we could take Ellen, whose mum had just gone into hospital. So naturally we said yes – even though my nan was staying with us, which meant me and Sam having to share a bedroom, which was very nearly DISASTER. See, I am a naturally quite tidy sort of person while Sam is just the opposite. After only three days, my bedroom had started to look like a tip. Sam and me had the biggest row of all time! I stuffed Sam's clothes up the chimney, and Sam called me a dingbat so then I chucked some of her stuff out of the window and it fell in the mud, and we fought each other all over the bedroom and pulled each other's hair out practically by the roots and yelled foul and disgusting things at each other.

Mum was distinctly cross with us. I could understand it, really, since a load of soot had come down the chimney and everything was covered in horrible black dust. Anyway, me and Sam made it up. We never stay cross for long!

We weren't very kind to Ellen just at first. We called her Droopy Drawers and got really mad at her when she used to follow us round and muck things up and make a nuisance of herself. Ellen was Special Needs, so we knew we had to make allowances, but, oh dear! She was *such* an embarrassment. (One time her knickers fell down in public and we just didn't know where to put ourselves!) But by the end we had grown quite fond of her and almost missed her when she went back home.

After Ellen had gone, we thought maybe we'd have some peace and quiet. Me and Sam, that is. We were worn out, what with all the fighting and screaming we'd done when we'd shared the room! And surely Mum ought to want a bit of a rest? I mean, she not only has to look after all of us kids, plus Dad, plus Jack and Daisy, who are our dogs, plus Felix, who is our cat, but she also has to do the accounts for Dad and answer the telephone and make appointments when people want him to go and do some plumbing for them. You'd have thought she'd welcome the chance to put her feet up. It's what she's always *saying* she wants to do.

But I think secretly my mum would have liked to be one of those people that have simply dozens and dozens of babies. Like the old woman that lived in the shoe. I think she really loves having the house full of children and animals and not having time to put her feet up. 'Cos guess what? Our first day back at school for the summer term, when Ellen had been gone for about *two weeks*, me and Sam got home to find Mum waiting for us in the kitchen with this little anxious smile hovering on her lips.

'Girls!' she said.

Me and Sam didn't say anything. We froze. It was just this feeling we had. Mum had gone and done it again! She'd gone and said yes! I thought, *I am not going to share my bedroom any more!* But of course Nan had gone back, so I wouldn't have to. Not unless Mum had agreed to foster a whole *family* of children.

But it wasn't a family. It was . . .

'A *boy*?' I shrieked.

'What's wrong with boys?' said Mum.

I thought of Gary Copestake and Charlie Potts. Sometimes there was a *lot* wrong with them.

'He's only little, isn't he?' I begged. 'Tell me he's only little!'

That was when Mum broke it to us: he was *twelve*.

Twelve is *not* little. Twelve is older than we were!

'That is just the pits!' I said. And I threw my school bag on to the table. 'The absolute *pits*!'

'The Radish will be twelve one day,' Mum reminded me.

'The Radish is different!'

'Oh?' said Mum. 'How?'

' 'Cos he's the Radish!'

Sam suddenly came to life.

'*Some* boys are OK,' she said.

'They're not!' I stamped across to the fridge. 'They're horrible! I can't stand them!'

We'd only been back at school one day and already Charlie Potts had accidentally-on-purpose trodden on my toe and Gary Copestake had flipped a rubber across the room and laughed when it bounced off my nose.

'Oh, Abi, really,' said Mum.

'I can't! I can't stand them! They're all right when they're little, and they're all right when they're old, but in between' – I reached into the fridge and helped myself to a strawberry yoghurt – 'in between they're the *pits*!'

'The way I see it,' said Mum, firmly, 'a child in need is a child in need whether it's a boy or a girl, no matter how old.'

'Is this boy in need?' said Sam.

'Any child is that has to be fostered. You know that,' said Mum.

'No, but I mean . . . *specially*. Abi, you pig!' Sam spun round, glaring at me. 'You're pinched the last strawberry yoghurt!'

'You'd have done the same if you'd got there first,' I said.

'*Ugh*! There's nothing but plain. I hate plain!'

'Put some sugar in it,' said Mum. 'And just stop complaining, the pair of you! You must be two of the most spoilt children on this planet.'

'Don't see how you can say that when you forced us to share a bedroom,' I muttered.

'That was for three short weeks!'

'Seemed like a lifetime. And anyhow, I thought we got to *say*.' I looked at Mum, accusingly. 'I thought we got to *say* whether we wanted someone to come.'

'It's only for a trial period.' Mum's voice was coaxing. She was obviously determined to have this horrible boy whether me and Sam liked it or not.

'What's a trial period?' said Sam.

'Well . . . just for a week or so, to see how he gets on. He won't be here all the time, in any case. He'll be away at school.'

'Away at school? You mean *boarding* school?' Sam pulled a face. 'Ugh! That means he's posh!'

'Nonsense!' said Mum. 'It means nothing of the kind.'

'Yes, it does.' Sam dipped a spoon in the sugar and stirred it vigorously into her yoghurt. Smugly I ate my strawberry one. 'Only rich kids go to boarding school.'

'And kids who don't get on too well with their step-dads.'

'Oh?' Sam perked up. 'Has he got a step-dad?'

'And a step-mum. His real mum and dad split up when he was a baby, then his mum got married again, only his new dad already had a family and Simon found it very difficult to fit in, so they sent him away to boarding school. Which *I* think,' said Mum, 'was a big mistake. The poor boy must feel totally unwanted.'

'So what's happened to his mum? His real mum?' Sam dumped another spoonful of sugar into her yoghurt. She'll get tooth rot, I thought.

'Well, it was really rather terrible. She was killed in a car crash, a couple of years ago. And now his step-dad's found another woman, and she and Simon don't get on at all. In fact, she's refused to have him in the house.'

'So we have to have him!'

'We don't *have* to. If you really feel as strongly as all that . . .'

There was a silence. I gave my empty yoghurt pot to Jack to lick out. Sam chomped on a spoonful of sugar.

'What about his dad?' I said. 'His real dad?'

'His dad's disappeared. No one knows where he is. They're still trying to trace him.'

I frowned.

More silence.

'I just thought,' said Mum, 'that it would be nice for him if he had somewhere to come at weekends. Otherwise he'll have to stay at school while everyone else goes home.'

I scowled rather fiercely at Jack, who had his nose in my yoghurt pot.

'Didn't think people at boarding schools went home.'

They didn't in any of the books I'd read. They stayed at school having midnight feasts in the dorm and going to church in crocodiles. That's what they did in the books I'd read.

Patiently, Mum explained that this particular school was really a day school.

'It just happens to take in a few boys as boarders. And most of them do go home at weekends. He'd be all by himself!'

I said, 'Why? Doesn't he have any friends he can go to?'

'Yeah, he's got to have friends!' said Sam.

But Mum said she didn't think he had. 'He's rather sad. A bit of a loner. He doesn't mix too well. He desperately needs someone to love him!'

Sam made a noise that sounded like 'Hmf!' I watched as Jack started to tear my yoghurt pot to pieces. (Jack likes destroying things. It's a doggy form of creativity.)

'Well?' said Mum.

I said, 'Well what?'

'Would you rather I told Miss Davies we've changed our mind?'

Did you notice the way she said *our* mind? She's always doing this to us! Making us feel mean. It's ever so unfair. She knows exactly how to get to us, my mum.

I heaved a sigh. Sam said, 'So long as we don't have to share again.'

'You won't have to share! He can have the spare room. It's only at weekends,' said Mum. 'And half term.'

'What about holidays?'

'We'll have to see about holidays when we get there. It may be that by that time things will have been sorted out with his step-mum. Either that or they'll have found his dad.'

'I think if people have families they ought to stay with them,' said Sam.

'We all think that,' agreed Mum. 'Unfortunately, things don't always work out as we'd like them to.'

No! Things certainly did not. I'd never imagined that we'd foster a *boy*. Not a great big thing of twelve.

'So when's he coming?' I said.

'Well, tomorrow, if you both agree.'

'*Tomorrow?*' Tomorrow was only Thursday. 'I thought you said at weekends?'

'It will be at weekends but he doesn't start back at school until Monday week.'

I received this news in deepest gloom.

'What's his name?' said Sam.

'Simon. Simon Spenser.'

Sam wrinkled her nose. '*Posh!*'

'Rubbish!' said Mum. 'It's a perfectly ordinary name. Don't be so ridiculous!'

'Sounds posh to me,' said Sam, and she chucked her yoghurt pot in the air for Daisy to catch.

'You two girls,' said Mum, 'have some most peculiar ideas.'

Huh! We weren't the only ones.

We discussed it later, when we were on our own.

'What about the Radish?' I wailed. 'Poor little Radish! Nobody asks *him*.'

'He's too young,' said Sam.

I looked at her, reprovingly. 'That's very ageist,' I said.

'Well, you were being sexist!'

'Yes, and you were being classist!'

We weren't quarrelling; we were just peeved that Mum hadn't sat us down and discussed things with us before going ahead and making her decision. 'Cos she *had* made a decision. She'd gone and told Miss Davies it was OK.

'Without even consulting us! I mean,' I said, 'we have to live here!'

'She'd have changed her mind if we'd really said no.'

'Yes, and then she'd have made us feel like scumbags!'

She wouldn't actually have said anything, but we'd know what she was thinking. This poor little lad – they were always little lads to Mum, even when they were twelve years old – this poor little lad with nowhere to go . . . how can Sam and Abi be so selfish?

I'd tried my best to feel properly sorry for him. I'd tried imagining how I would feel if so many terrible things had happened to me. But all I could think of was, I don't want a *boy* in the house!

'It'll be all right,' said Sam, 'so long as he's not posh.'

'It *won't* be all right! It'll be horrid! Who wants a *boy* clumping round the place?'

'Sexist!' taunted Sam.

'Classist!' I retorted.

'Well, anyway, I don't expect he'll have anything much to do with us. Unless, of course . . .' Sam brightened.

'Unless what?'

'Unless he might like to play football with me!'

Sam was always looking for people to play

football with her. The Radish was too young and Dad was too old and I was absolutely useless. Even Jack was better than I was!

'I wouldn't mind that,' said Sam.

My heart went thudding right down to my shoes. I immediately had these visions of Sam spending all her time with Simon, kicking a ball about in the back garden. Instead of me and Sam mooching round the shops together on a Sunday morning, it would be Sam and Simon up the park playing football. I'd never see anything of Sam at all!

'Maybe he won't like animals,' I said. 'And then he'll have to go.'

Nobody could live in our house and not like animals. Maybe he'd be allergic to them. They'd bring him out in spots or make him wheeze. Maybe I should capture Felix and shut him up in the spare bedroom so he'd leave lots of cat hairs . . .

I didn't, of course, 'cos Felix wouldn't let me. He is a most *contrary* animal! He'd yowled and yowled to get into that bedroom when Nan was with us. Now he yowled and yowled to get out of it.

'What's the matter with that cat?' said Mum. 'Where is he? Has someone locked him in somewhere?' She stood, with her head to one side. 'It sounds as if he's in the spare bedroom! Gus, run up and let him out, there's a good boy.'

Two seconds later the Radish came downstairs carrying a triumphant Felix in his arms. So that was *one* plan that didn't work out.

And after that it was too late. We got home from school on Thursday afternoon and there he was . . . *Simon.*

2

I'd already made up my mind I was going to hate him. In class that day I'd had to sit next to a boy called Mark Arthur who'd made a rude noise, I mean a *really* rude noise, right in the middle of our silent reading period. Everyone started giggling and you'll never guess what he did! Or maybe you will if you have any boys like him in your school. He pinched his nose between finger and thumb and pointed at *me*. And I turned bright red, even though I wasn't the one that had done it. So then of course everyone thought that I *had* done it, and that made me go even redder. And afterwards, in the playground, Gary Copestake and Charlie Potts came and danced round me holding their noses and going 'Ugh! What a pong!'

I know girls can be horrid in lots of ways but they are never horrid like that.

'Just ignore them,' said Sam. 'They're not worth bothering with.' And then she added, 'But I'll bash them if you like!'

I was almost tempted, only I didn't want to get Sam into trouble.

'*Boys*,' I muttered.

Sam knew what I was thinking of.

'He mightn't be too bad,' she said.

I just said, 'Huh!'

And then we got home, and there he was. Waiting for us in the kitchen with Mum. I took one look at him and went bright red all over again. I do *hate* it when this happens! It makes me look like some kind of human tomato. But there I was, expecting a clone of Gary Copestake (or Charlie Potts. Even worse!) and here was this absolutely drop dead gorgeous boy, smiling at me across the kitchen.

My knees just went to water!!!

I suppose I ought to try and describe him, though I am not, unfortunately, very good at descriptions. I know it is not enough to just say that he was tall, dark and handsome – though that is what he was! You have to say poetical things such as 'His dark wavy hair rippled like waves on the seashore' or 'His eyes were like twin pools of black treacle'. Stuff like that. I can never find the right words.

He wasn't a bit like Gary Copestake. Or Charlie Potts. Or Mark Arthur. Or any of the other boys in our class. In spite of only being a year older, he looked really sophisticated.

Mum said, 'Abi . . . Sam . . . Gus! This is Simon.'

Simon held out his hand and said, 'Hi.' And since the Radish didn't seem to know what to do, and Sam seemed, like, frozen, I was the one who took it and said 'Hi' back to him.

'He's already met the animals, you'll be glad to know,' said Mum. She opened the back door and Jack and Daisy came bounding in. As usual, they hurled themselves at us.

'Wow!' said Simon. 'What a greeting!'

Usually when we get home from school, if it's

not dark, me and Sam have to take the dogs up the park for their second walk, but Mum said that today we needn't bother.

'Simon got here early, so we've already taken them. Isn't that nice?'

I beamed.

'I thought that would please you!' said Mum. She turned to Simon. 'They're always moaning about having to take the dogs out when they get home from school.'

'We don't!' said Sam.

'Oh, no?' said Mum. 'I seem to remember, only yesterday—'

'That was different! There was something I wanted to watch on telly. It'll confuse them if other people start taking them out.'

'They had a great time,' said Simon. 'Daisy saw off a Rottweiler.'

'A *Rottweiler*?' Sam almost screeched it at him. 'You shouldn't have let her anywhere near a Rottweiler! It could have killed her!'

'It was a *dog*,' said Mum. 'It was quite safe. A

dog wouldn't attack a bitch.'

'What about Jack? It might have gone for Jack!'

'Well, it didn't! It was perfectly friendly. What are you making all this fuss for?'

I had been wondering that, too. It wasn't like Sam to fuss. Jack and Daisy talk to all sorts of dogs when we take them out. There's never any trouble. One of Jack's best friends is a big bull terrier called Butch, who looks really scary. But he's a great pudding! We also know some Rotties and an Irish Wolfhound. I couldn't understand what Sam's problem was.

'They're used to going out with *us*,' she said.

'Well, all right,' said Mum. 'Tomorrow, you and Abi can take them. And I don't want any moaning!'

We all sat down at the kitchen table to have tea. I couldn't help noticing that Simon had really classy table manners. Poor old Ellen had slopped and slurped and dribbled things, and the Radish was still at the messy stage, and even Sam had a tendency to bolt her food. I mean, Sam just

22

naturally does everything fast. I am quite slow. Quite snail-like.

I suppose perhaps I am a bit *meticulous*. Sam would say pernickety. (It was the reason we had the mega-row over the state she'd got my bedroom into.) I really like things to be nice! I don't think even Mum cares as much as I do. She always says quite cheerfully that she is 'slapdash and happy'.

So I was probably the only one who really appreciated the way Simon cut up his food into little bits instead of gobbling, and chewed with his mouth shut instead of churning everything about like a cement mixer (I hate it when you can see all the food going round in great gobbets), and waited till he'd finished eating before he started to speak. I was dead impressed! I immediately took my elbows off the table and sat up straight, just to show him that we weren't all a load of slobs.

After tea we went to watch some telly, but there wasn't very much on and the Radish got bored and wanted us to play with him.

'*Pleethe*, Abi! *Pleethe!*'

I groaned inwardly and said, 'What do you want to play?'

The Radish said, 'Thnaketh 'n' Ladderth!' and this time I groaned out loud because Snakes & Ladders was what he always said. That or Snap. They are both the sort of game, when you have played them about a thousand times you feel there is not much more to be got out of them.

'Can't you think of anything else?' said Sam.

'No!' The Radish made fists of his hands and pummelled at his cheeks. 'I want Thnaketh 'n' Ladderth!'

'I am *bored* with Snakes & Ladders! And anyway,' said Sam, 'I'm watching television.'

The Radish's face puckered.

'Wouldn't you like to go into the garden and ride your bike?' I said.

Slowly, the Radish shook his head.

'It's all right,' said Simon. 'I'll play. Where's the board? Go and get the board!'

So then, of course, I felt incredibly mean and had to join in, but it wasn't so bad playing with Simon 'cos he kept up a string of jokey comments which made me laugh. He made the Radish laugh, too.

'Oops!' he'd go. 'What's this?'

And the Radish would cry, 'It'th a thnake!'

'A snake . . . help, help! It's trying to gobble me up!'

'You've got to thlide down it.'

'Oh! Right. Off we go . . . down and round, down and round, down and – does this snake never end?'

Or if he came to a ladder it was, 'Watch out, you guys! I'm on my way! Here I come . . . wheee! Up the ladder!'

Sam, who was still glued to the television, kept huffing and puffing and making scoffing noises. I suppose it *was* a bit childish, but it kept the Radish amused. I didn't see what call Sam had to sneer.

After our third game of Snakes & Ladders

Mum came in and announced that it was time the Radish had his bath. Phew! What a relief. I think even Simon was beginning to feel the strain.

'The Radish would go on all evening,' I said.

'I remember when I was his age,' said Simon, 'I got this thing about a computer game – Aliens in Space. I played it over and over! I just couldn't stop. It was like I was obsessed.'

'I get obsessed,' I said. 'Like I can't stop reading the same book or listening to the same bit of music. Last year I read this one book *ten times*.'

'Gosh,' said Simon.

Sam's head whipped round from the telly. I made a gargoyle face at her.

'In the end,' I said, 'I knew it off by heart.'

We packed the Snakes & Ladders away in its box. The box was all tatty by now, the game had been in and out so often.

'Your mum says you've got a dolls' house,' said Simon.

'Yes.' I stiffened. Was he going to jeer at me?

Dolls' houses are girls' stuff. Boys can be ever so snooty about girls' stuff.

'She says you like to make things for it.'

'Yes, I do,' I said. 'I like to make furniture and decorate the walls and plan colour schemes.' Defiantly I added, 'It's what I'm going to do when I grow up.'

'Decorate dolls' houses?' said Simon.

I looked at him, sharply, but he wasn't poking fun.

'No!' I said. 'Decorate *real* houses.'

'Oh, so you're practising for later on.'

I nodded, gratefully. He had understood! It wasn't just a game. It was serious.

'I'm good at making things,' said Simon. 'I made some bookshelves last term. Maybe I could make something for your dolls' house?'

I scrambled eagerly to my feet.

'D'you want to come and see it?'

Together we went up to my bedroom, leaving Sam to watch her boring old telly. I didn't know what the matter was with Sam. She wasn't being her usual bright and bubbly self. But just for the moment, I couldn't be bothered. Simon wanted to see my dolls' house!

I was specially proud of it right then 'cos I'd spent the Easter holidays putting up new wallpaper. It looked dead smart! I'd also put in some new carpet. I'd found the carpet in a skip at the end of the road. Someone had been clearing out a house and they'd thrown away this perfectly good rug. Well, it was a bit threadbare in the middle, but all round the edge it was still OK. So I took it home with me and cut it up. Sam said I was mad and that it was probably stealing, but I didn't see how it could be. I mean, it was only being thrown away.

I told Simon about it, and he didn't think I was mad. Or that it was stealing.

'You have to use whatever you can get hold of. Have you ever thought of doing a garden?'

'A garden? I'm not very good at gardening. And anyway Mum says we can't really do very much with ours because of the dogs.'

'No, I mean for the dolls' house . . . a garden for the dolls' house.'

'Oh!' I'd never thought of that. 'A *real* garden?'

'Well, you could make it look like one.'

'How?'

'What you want,' said Simon, 'is a wooden frame . . . I could make you a wooden frame! I could do it tomorrow, if your dad would let me use his tools.'

I said that I was sure Dad would. He's very easy-going, my dad. He lets us do most anything. It's Mum who sometimes goes on the warpath. When Mum is mad, BEWARE!

But they were Dad's tools, not Mum's, so I didn't see any problem.

Me and Simon spent the rest of the time before supper planning what we were going to do to make the garden. Simon was going to make the frame and put a little gate in it. He was also going to make a little archway. I was going to make flower pots out of thimbles, and flowers out of coloured tissue paper to put in them, and also to climb up the archway.

'What about grass?'

'Crazy-paving would be better,' said Simon.

'We could go into the garden and collect pebbles!'

'Yes, and you could have a patio, and a table and chairs, and one of those little umbrella things they give you in burger places when you have an ice cream sundae.'

'And a swing! We could have a swing! We could make a swing, couldn't we?'

'Absolutely,' said Simon.

'And then when we've done a back garden we can do a front one, as well!'

I was really excited at the thought of making a garden. If Simon could do all the big stuff – like the frame – I would do all the small, fiddly things like the flowers. I love doing things like that!

'What about Sam?' said Simon. 'Will she want to be in on it?'

'Dunno.' I crinkled my nose. Once upon a time, when she had first come to us, Sam had seemed quite interested in my dolls' house. She had even helped me redecorate it. She had done the bottom half and I had done the top, and the colours she had chosen had been all bright and bold, just like Sam herself, and I could hardly bear to look at them 'cos privately I thought they were vulgar. I don't mean Sam is vulgar; but I didn't want my dolls' house all purple and orange and yucky sick yellow! I wanted it mint green and lime, and blush pink and honey. I wanted it to be *tasteful*; only Sam said that was boring.

But anyway, it was ages since Sam had taken any notice of the dolls' house. I didn't think, probably, that she would want to help us.

'What sort of things does Sam like doing?' said Simon.

'She likes walking the dogs. She likes going to gym classes. She likes . . .' I hesitated. 'She likes playing football. When she can find anyone to play with her.'

I waited for Simon to say, 'I'll play with her!'

Instead he pulled a face and said, 'I'm not really into football.'

'Aren't you?' I said.

'No.' He pushed a lock of hair off his forehead. It killed me when he did that! He had this bit of hair that kept flopping over his eyes and he had to keep flicking it back. 'We do rugby at school. That's even worse.'

'Is it?' I gazed at him, sympathetically. 'We only do netball. That's bad enough.'

'Games are such a bore,' said Simon.

'They are,' I said, 'aren't they? Specially when you're not much good at them.'

'What about the Radish?'

'He's too little. And he gets scared very easily. It's not his fault! His mum's boyfriend used to knock him about. He was terrified when he first came to us. He's loads better now but he's still rather fragile.' That was what Mum said: the Radish was *fragile*. 'You have to be really careful how you treat him.'

'I'll be careful,' promised Simon.

'It's just that loud voices or anything . . . he gets very easily upset. We're hoping we can adopt him soon,' I said. 'Then I'll have a brother *and* a sister!'

'Is Sam adopted?'

'No, she's a foster. But her and me, we're the same as sisters.'

'Did you want to have a sister?'

'Mmm!' I nodded. 'See, I was an only child before.'

'I'm an only child,' said Simon.

I fell silent, chewing on my thumb. I remembered Mum telling us how Simon's mum had got married again and how his new dad had already got children of his own and how Simon didn't get on with them. I thought perhaps all this talk of brothers and sisters might be upsetting for him, so as hastily as I could I changed the subject.

'Let's go down and see if Dad's in yet! Then we can ask him about the tools.'

Dad said that of course Simon could borrow

his tools. I knew that he would!

'I'll be extra careful with them,' said Simon.

'That's all right,' said Dad. 'They're there to be used. Just don't go hammering any nails into yourself or chopping off any fingers.'

'I wouldn't do that,' said Simon. 'I'm good at woodwork.'

I looked at Sam as he said this. Sam was quite good at woodwork, too. I wondered if she might offer to help, but she didn't say anything. It was Mum who asked what we were going to make.

'We're going to make a garden for my dolls' house,' I said.

'And where exactly are you planning to keep this garden?'

'Upstairs. In my bedroom.'

'Well, I just hope Felix doesn't take it into his head to use it as a lavatory!'

'Mum! Of course he won't,' I said.

Really, Mum was so rude! And in front of Simon, too! He wasn't that sort of boy at all. He wasn't in the least like Gary Copestake or Charlie Potts. *Or* Mark Arthur, with his horrid stinky noises. He was gentle and sensitive and interesting. And he didn't like football!

At bedtime, Sam came in with Daisy to sit on my bed while we drank our hot chocolate.

'Simon's really nice,' I said, 'isn't he?'

Sam just grunted and humped a shoulder.

'He's not a bit like Gary Copestake.'

Sam still didn't say anything.

'I asked him, but I'm afraid he doesn't play football.'

'No, well, he wouldn't, would he?' said Sam. Her lip curled. 'He probably prefers *croquet*!'

'What's crokey?'

'CRO-kay.' Sam stood up and made swishing movements.

'Oh, I know!' I said. 'Where you hit balls through hoops.'

'Yeah. *Balls* through *hoops*.'

'What makes you think he'd like doing that?'

'Well! *Gosh*.' Sam flicked at an imaginary bit

of hair. I regarded her solemnly over the rim of my hot chocolate mug.

'Don't you like him?'

'He's all right,' said Sam.

But I knew that wasn't really what she thought.

'What's wrong with him?' I said.

'He's posh,' muttered Sam. 'And he's *smarmy*,' she added, as she left the room.

I didn't think he was posh or smarmy. I thought he was lovely.

I did hope Sam wasn't going to be jealous.

3

Saturday morning we took the dogs up the park, same as we always do. I didn't think, probably, that Simon would want to come with us. Sam wasn't being exactly friendly to him, and the Radish, after all, was only seven and still a bit of a baby. As for me, I know I am not in the least bit glamorous or exciting – especially when I am dressed for taking the dogs out! It was wet and muddy in the park and I think you'd have to be someone like Madonna or someone to look glamorous in an old shabby anorak and clumping great wellies! Plus it didn't help that I still wore my hair in plaits. I was beginning to feel that that was rather a childish thing to do. Except that when I tried *un*plaiting it, it just sort of . . . hung about. All limp and manky and horrible. So I pulled it back in a bunch and put an elastic band round it and hoped that that looked a bit more sophisticated.

I think it must have done! 'Cos as soon as he saw me and Sam in our anoraks Simon said, 'Oh, good! Are you taking the dogs out? Can I come with you?'

Sam scowled. She did! She *scowled*. Fortunately Simon didn't see, 'cos he was already rushing upstairs to change his shoes. But I scowled back at her and said, 'What's your problem?' To which she simply pulled a face and went stalking off with her head in the air.

My heart sank. I didn't want Sam being jealous! It was true that I'd been worried, before Simon came, that he and Sam might go off playing football all by themselves and leave me behind; and then, I expect, I would have been the one to be jealous. But this was different! Me and Simon weren't doing things together. We were doing them with Sam and the Radish and the dogs. Well, I suppose we were doing the dolls' house garden together, but Sam could have joined in if she'd wanted! No one was stopping her. She just wasn't interested.

We walked up to the park with Simon and me in the lead, with Jack. Jack pulls all the way. He gets so excited! Sam and the Radish followed behind, with Daisy. Daisy never pulls. She's more of an ambling sort of dog. But as a rule Sam makes sure she keeps up. She was only hanging back 'cos she didn't want to walk with Simon.

Jack was doing his usual tug tug tug all up the road. He doesn't know how to walk normally, that dog. He only has these little legs, but they flash along so fast you can hardly see them move. The lead is always at full stretch. It's a wonder my arms don't hang down to my ankles, the way he yanks at them.

Simon could see what was happening. Well, anyone could.

'Would you like me to take him for you?' he said.

Wow! I was really knocked out by that. I'm not used to boys being polite! Once at school Miss Mallard told Gary Copestake to help one of the girls move a heavy table, and you'll never guess what he said. He said, 'Why should I? She's a fem'nist. She can move it herself.' Miss Mallard didn't half give him what for! She said it was nothing to do with feminism. 'It's a question of good manners.'

Simon had lovely manners! Yesterday he'd gone shopping with Mum and had insisted on carrying her bags to the car for her. Mum was so impressed she'd told us all about it.

'You don't meet with that kind of old-world courtesy these days. He even held the door open for people! I must say, I rather like it.'

Me, too! But old grumpy Sam didn't. She just did her scowling act and muttered things under her breath.

'He's poncy,' she said.

Well! I didn't care about Sam. I let Simon take Jack and tried not to hear the scoffing noise that came from behind me. Sam was being a real pain.

We had a wonderful walk! We went to parts of

the park we don't usually go to, like the woody bit behind the football pitches and the old chalk pit near the children's playground. Jack chased sticks and Daisy groffled, and they both got covered all over in mud and so did the rest of us. Simon had set out looking really cool in a navy tracksuit and a pair of trainers that Sam would have killed for. He got covered in mud, too! But he didn't seem to mind.

'A dirty dog is a happy dog,' he said. 'Isn't that right?' He held out his hand to Jack, but Jack just flattened his ears and backed away.

'*Jack!*' I said. 'What's the matter with you?'

He's usually a very friendly dog. Too friendly, Mum says. He'll go up to anyone and say hello! But he wouldn't go to Simon.

'Here, boy!' Simon put a hand in his pocket and brought out a bar of Twix. 'Want a bit of chocolate?'

'They're not allowed to eat chocolate,' said Sam. 'It's bad for them.'

'One teeny little piece won't hurt,' I said.

'Yes, it will! It'll rot his teeth.'

Sam was a fine one to talk. *I'd* seen her, feeding jelly beans to Daisy. But anyway, Jack wouldn't take the chocolate. I could see that he wanted it; but he wouldn't take it.

'See? He knows what's good for him,' said Sam.

'What about Daisy?'

'No!' Sam lunged at Daisy and pulled her away. 'It'll make her fat.'

What cheek! After feeding her half a pack of jelly beans.

Simon's face fell. I felt really sorry for him. I couldn't think what was making Jack behave so oddly. I mean, he *adores* chocolate! I don't let him have too much, but even just a tiny crumb is a treat.

'I'm going to eat it,' said Simon. He popped it in his mouth. 'Yum yum!'

Jack took up a position behind my legs and just looked at him.

'Well, suit yourself,' said Simon.

He was pretending not to care, but I could see that he was hurt. I'd have been hurt, too. It's very upsetting when you try to make friends with someone's dog and they refuse to talk to you.

Apologetically, I said that it was probably because Simon was a stranger.

'See, we've trained them not to take food from people they don't know.'

Sam choked. I glared at her. It was the Radish, in all innocence, who piped up, 'Auntie' (Auntie is what he calls Mum) 'Auntie theth he'th a human duthtbin . . . she theth he'll eat anything he can find.'

'Ah, yes,' I said quickly. 'Anything he can *find*. But not if a stranger gives it to him.'

The Radish opened his mouth. I knew what he was going to say. He was going to say that only last week, in the park, a woman we'd never seen before had offered Jack a dog biscuit and he'd followed her all the way to the gates begging for more! Fortunately, Simon got in first.

'How long will it be before I stop being a stranger?'

'Oh . . . not long! Just a—'

'Few months, probably!' Sam clipped Daisy's lead on and seized the Radish by the hand. 'It's time to go! We've been out for ages.'

I did wish she wouldn't be so horrible to poor Simon. He was trying really hard! He couldn't help going to boarding school and having nice manners and speaking like Prince Charles. Well, he didn't *exactly* speak like Prince Charles, I mean he didn't sound all strangled and say things like 'ite' instead of 'out', which I have noticed is what the Royal Family do. But he didn't speak like Gary Copestake, either! In any case, people can't help the way they speak and I don't think it should be held against them.

On our way out of the park we bumped into Mary-Jo Mitchell and her friend Lissie Thomas. Usually if they meet us when we've got the dogs, and especially if the dogs are all wet and muddy, they cross over to the other side of the road and wave at us from there. They don't like dogs (which is one of the reasons I don't like them). Today, because Simon was with us, they stayed where they were. In fact they stopped slap, bang, right in front of us. In front of me and Simon, that is. They didn't bother with Sam and the Radish.

'Hi, Abi!' said Mary-Jo.

I said, 'Hi,' and made to walk on, but they were all over the pavement, blocking our way. Mary-Jo was simpering and Lissie's eyes were, like, bulging in their sockets.

'Aren't you going to introduce us?' breathed Mary-Jo.

'This is Simon,' I said. And then as an afterthought, 'This is Mary-Jo and this is Lissie.'

'Hi,' said Simon; and he brushed that lock of hair off his forehead.

It really killed me when he did that! It killed them, too. I could almost see Mary-Jo going weak at the knees, and Lissie's eyes were out on stalks. They were obviously dying to know more!

'I'm afraid we're in a hurry,' I said. 'I've got to go to my art class.'

They sprang off the kerb as me and Jack went past, but they weren't quite quick enough. Jack managed to bounce up and blob them with his dirty paws! He got Lissie first and she screeched fit to bust. Then as I yanked him away he jumped up at Mary-Jo and got her, as well. She screeched even louder!

'Sorry,' I cried. 'Just let it dry, it'll brush off!'

I went on my way feeling what I can only describe as a glow. I don't mean because Jack had splatted them both with mud (although I did think it was quite funny and so would anyone that knows them). The glow was because they had seen me with Simon, and because Lissie's eyes had come out on stalks and Mary-Jo had gone weak at the knees. She had sort of . . . wobbled, and had had to clutch at Lissie to steady herself. I hoped they might think he was my boyfriend, though unfortunately everyone at school knows we are a foster family, so most likely they would have guessed the truth. All the same, they had seen him walking with me! With *me*, not with Sam! Even though Sam is heaps prettier than I am, at least I think she is.

But she is not pretty when she scowls, and she had been doing a *lot* of scowling these last couple of days.

I turned back to see Mary-Jo and Lissie hysterically scrubbing at themselves with their hankies.

'I told them to leave it,' I said. 'They'll just make it worse. It brushes off quite easily once it's dry. It's only a bit of mud!'

'Who are they, anyway?' said Simon.

'Oh, just a couple of grots from school.'

Grot was our latest word. Grots were people who screamed when little innocent dogs jumped up to say hello. (Also people who don't like foxes visiting their gardens, and people who complain about pigeons making a mess, and people who put down traps to kill mice. *Those* sort of people. They are all grots.)

'I can't stand it,' I said, 'when people are stupid with dogs. I mean, it's not as if they're man-eating sharks or anything.'

'I expect even man-eating sharks can be quite lovable,' said Simon. 'To other man-eating sharks, that is.'

I beamed at him. He was definitely *not* a grot!

Up in front, the Radish was beginning to lag. This was because Sam was tugging at him, trying to keep her distance from me and Simon.

'She oughtn't to drag him like that,' I said. 'He's only little!'

'Shall I give him a carry? Hey, Radish!' Simon went striding off, all manfully, towards them. I heard my heart go 'Ping!' inside my chest. 'Fancy a piggy back?'

The Radish's face broke into a big smile. 'Yeth pleethe!'

He rode home on Simon's shoulders, proud as punch. Sam waited for me to catch up with her.

'Trying to worm his way in,' she muttered.

I said, 'He just felt sorry for the Radish, that's all. The way you were yanking him.'

'Yeah, well, we've got to get home. You'll be late for your class.'

From twelve o'clock to one o'clock, I had my art class. It was held in the local technical college, and Dad always drove me there and picked me up afterwards. Then in the afternoon Sam went to her gym class, just up the road in the church hall. Today Mum said that she would come and pick me up because Dad was doing a plumbing job on the other side of town.

'And I thought it might be a good opportunity to buy you some summer clothes.'

Well! Normally I wouldn't have been terribly interested in buying clothes as I am not really a clothes sort of person. I mean, I am not what you would call fashion conscious. Not like Mary-Jo and Lissie. They wouldn't be seen dead, for instance, in a skirt that wasn't exactly the right length. Just at the moment, the right length was about two inches below the bum. So of course

49

you had to wear tights, and they had to be the right *sort* of tights; in other words black and shiny, made out of that stretchy stuff called Lycra.

My skirts all reached down to just above my knee (dead naff) and the only tights I had were brown ribbed ones (even naffer). But I didn't care! I had other things to think about, like . . . well! The dogs. And my dolls' house. And making the garden. Mum said it was refreshing to have a ten year old (ten and three quarters, actually) who wasn't 'obsessed with the way she looked'.

'I know this isn't your idea of fun,' she said, as she whisked me off to Hamlyn's, the big department store in the shopping centre, 'but we'll do it as quickly as possible and then we can go and have a cream tea. How about that?'

'Brilliant,' I said. 'Where's the Radish?'

'Oh, he's happy at home, with Simon. I left them out in the garden.' She laughed. 'When I asked him what they were doing he told me it was a guy kind of thing.'

I giggled. The thought of the Radish doing 'a guy kind of thing!'

'Simon is so good with him,' said Mum. 'There aren't many twelve year olds who'd bother with a little lad of Gus's age.'

'Sam doesn't like him,' I said, regretfully.

'No, well, Sam's being a bit silly. She'll get over it. Now, let's go and find something for you to wear.'

I ended up with two tops, two skirts, two pairs of shiny black tights and a pair of trainers. I chose them all! I think Mum was quite surprised. She hadn't expected me to show that much interest. We had a bit of a tussle over the skirts.

'They're nice,' said Mum, 'but far too short! Let's see if they've got them in a longer length.'

'Mum, no!' I wailed. 'These are dead right!'

'But there's hardly anything of them!' said Mum.

'That's the way skirts are, these days,' I said.

'Really,' said Mum.

'Really,' I said.

Mum shook her head. 'Your dad will have a fit!'

'Dad won't even notice,' I said.

Mum had to admit that I was right. Dad's got a wonderful eye for a U-bend or a stop-cock, but he doesn't know the first thing about fashion! It's a big joke in our family that one time when he and Mum were going out to some posh dinner, he looked at Mum rather nervously and said, 'You don't think that dress is a bit . . . skimpy, do you, my love?'

'This dress,' said Mum, 'happens to be my *slip*.'

Dad can't even tell the difference between a dress and a slip! He'd never notice the length of my skirt.

'It's what everyone's wearing,' I said to Mum.

'Not me!' said Mum. 'But there you go, I guess I'm just an old fuddy-duddy.'

While we were in the shopping centre I bought some thimbles to make flower pots out of for my garden, and some packets of crinkly paper, all different colours, to make the flowers with. I had to get thimbles with flat bottoms, so they would stand upright. I explained that I wanted them as flower pots, and the lady who was serving us smiled kindly at me as if she thought I was a bit simple. But I am used to people doing that. It doesn't worry me. They don't know that one day I am going to be a famous interior designer, 'by appointment to Her Majesty'!

When we got home, Dad was still out but Sam had just come in. Simon and the Radish were in the garden doing their guy kind of thing, whatever that was. I didn't go out to see, 'cos I wanted to rush upstairs and try on my new clothes. Sam came with me.

'Cool,' she said, as I peacocked round in one of my new tops and short skirts. 'But you'll have to do something about your hair!'

I started to say, 'Do you think I should get it—' when from somewhere in the garden came the sound of unearthly yowling. Me and Sam sprang to the window, but we couldn't see anything.

'It sounded like Felix!'

Sam turned and shot from the room. Together we tore down the stairs and burst out into the garden. Mum was there before us. We were just in time to see the tail end of Felix, disappearing over the wall.

'What happened?' shrieked Sam.

'What did you do to him?' cried Mum.

'I'm sorry.' Simon's face had turned a ghostly kind of white. 'It was my fault.'

'Why?' said Mum. 'What happened?'

'We made a bow and arrow, and the Radish . . .'

We all turned to look at the Radish.

'He shot an arrow at him,' whispered Simon.

'Oh, Radish! How could you?' I raced at breakneck speed across the flower bed, not caring about my lovely new skirt (or the flowers). 'Felix! Felix!' I called. 'Where are you? Come here, Felix! Please!'

But Felix wouldn't. He had been frightened

and he was lying low. No matter how we called and coaxed, he refused to come.

'He didn't mean to hurt him,' said Simon. 'He didn't realise! Did you?'

Slowly and tearfully, the Radish shook his head. His thumb was in his mouth and his face, unlike Simon's, had turned bright red.

'You shouldn't ever, ever shoot an arrow at a person or an animal,' said Simon. 'But it's my fault! I should have told him.'

'You weren't to know,' said Mum. 'But perhaps a bow and arrow isn't the wisest toy for a seven year old. Shall we put it away somewhere safe?'

'Yeth.' The Radish nodded. He held out the bow for Mum to take. Then he burst into tears and said, 'He'th not deaded, ith he?'

'Who knows?' muttered Sam, and she hurled herself at the wall, pulled herself up to the top of it and sprang down into next door's garden. *Mrs Pink's* garden. Mrs Pink is an animal hater. We couldn't leave poor frightened Felix in Mrs Pink's garden! Especially as we didn't know how badly injured he was.

I rushed and got a flower pot – a proper one – and stood it against the fence so I could climb on top of it and see what Sam was up to. She was crawling on her hands and knees, peering into Mrs Pink's flower beds.

'Shall I call round,' said Simon, 'and ask if I can go and help look?'

'Yes, all right,' said Mum. She was busy comforting the Radish. 'Mind you apologise! She's rather prickly.'

'I'll come with you,' I said.

'No!' Mum grabbed hold of me. 'Let Simon do it.'

Me and Mrs Pink, and Mrs Pink and Sam, had all 'had words'. So probably Mum was wise, sending Simon on his own. All the same, it was terrible just having to stand and wait, not being able to do anything. Mum wouldn't even let me perch on my flower pot, for fear of upsetting Mrs Pink.

The poor little Radish was weeping his heart out. He is such a gentle little boy! I knew he wouldn't ever do anything on purpose to hurt Felix. I was terrified that maybe Felix might have been so badly injured that he had crawled away to die, which is the sort of thing that cats do. He could be dying right now, in Mrs Pink's garden, amongst all her rotten flowers that she's always going on about. And then I heard Sam cry, 'Felix!' and my heart almost stopped beating. A few seconds later she yelled, 'I've got him!'

I rushed back to my flower pot. I didn't care about Mrs Pink.

'Is he all right?' I quavered.

'Dunno,' said Sam.

We all rushed into the house. Mum threw open the front door as Sam came marching up the path, followed by Simon. In her arms, she was cradling Felix.

'Let me have him,' said Mum.

Mum took him into the sitting room and carefully examined him all over, and oh the relief!

He'd only been frightened; not actually hurt.

'Give him a stroke,' Mum told the Radish. 'Go on!'

Very timidly, the Radish stretched out a hand. I'm sure he thought that Felix was either going to run away from him or scratch. But Felix didn't do either. He is a really good cat! He let the Radish pick him up and cuddle him, just as if nothing had ever happened.

'There you are,' said Mum. 'He doesn't bear grudges.'

Felix didn't; but Sam did. That night when we were drinking our hot chocolate she went on and on and on about it until I felt like screaming.

'It was *his* fault. It's no good blaming the Radish.'

'I'm not blaming the Radish,' I said.

'Fancy giving him a bow and arrow!'

'It was a guys kind of thing.'

'Guys kind of thing!' Sam looked at me, contemptuously. '*Shooting cats?*'

'He didn't mean to! It was an accident.'

'He could have killed him! He could have put his eye out! He could have . . .'

On and on and *on*.

'You're being unfair,' I said. 'Just 'cos Simon speaks nicely and has nice manners!'

'That's got nothing to do with it.'

'Yes, it has! You think he's posh.'

'Well, he is.'

'So what? He can't help it.'

'Oh, I'm going to bed,' said Sam.

It was quite a relief. When Sam gets going, she is like a *bulldozer*.

I heard her stamping off down the passage. I heard her open her bedroom door. And then I heard it SLAM behind her. She was in a right mood!

4

To my enormous great surprise, when we came out of school on Monday afternoon we found Simon waiting for us at the school gates! He had the Radish with him. He was holding him by the hand. As soon as he saw us, the Radish broke away and came running towards us, going 'Abi, Abi! Sam!' He's used to us going down to the Infants to collect him, so I expect he got a bit fussed when Simon turned up instead. He's very easily worried by things, is the Radish. He probably thought something had happened to us, or that he was being taken away to a new home. Mum says he's still quite insecure.

'Had a good day?' said Simon. That was the way he talked. Like a grown-up. It killed me! He was really sophisticated. Sam, of course, just thought it was posh, and turned her nose up.

'Ai've hed a parfickly *splendid* day,' she

drawled. 'Thenk you *so* much for asking!' And then, in her normal voice, she added, 'But Abi hasn't. Have you?'

I frowned. I didn't want Simon knowing the horrible time I'd had.

'Abi's had a *bad* day.'

'Really?' said Simon. He sounded so sympathetic! And then he flipped his lock of hair and my heart went *boing*. 'Really really?'

I nodded, gloomily. It was Gary Copestake and Charlie Potts. As usual. They'd been giving me a whole load of hassle, wanting to know where the pigtails had gone.

'Cat got the pigtails? Where's the pigtails?'

What I'd done, I'd twisted my plaits on top of my head and fixed them with a hairslide. It looked really neat! Even Dad had noticed. He said, 'My! We're becoming very grand all of a sudden. What's brought this on? Or shouldn't I ask?'

Needless to say, I went red as a raspberry. But good old Mum came to the rescue!

'Nothing's brought it on,' she said. 'She's nearly eleven. She's growing up. Doesn't want to look like a little girl any more, do you, pet?'

'Well, it suits her,' said Dad. 'I'll say that!'

But those two horrible boys had to go and ruin it all. Gary Copestake came tearing past me, yanking at my hairslide so that the slide came undone and my plaits fell down and stuck out sideways, looking utterly ridiculous. Next thing I know, Charlie Potts is racing up behind me and grabbing a plait in each hand and going, 'Ding dong! Anyone at home?'

When I'd tried to put the slide back I found that it was broken, so for the rest of the morning I had to sit in class with plaits sticking out on either side of my head and all the boys going 'Ding dong! Ding dong!' and tugging at them whenever Miss Mallard had her back turned. In the end I'd twisted them both together on top of my head with the same elastic band, but that didn't work 'cos halfway through the afternoon they started slipping backwards and before I knew it I'd got this plaited hoop hanging down the back of my neck. Of course you can guess what Gary and Charlie did to *that*.

'Hey!' yelled Gary. 'Get a handle on this!' And he starts yanking at me, with one hand through the hoop. Which then, of course, came apart, so that I had one plait sticking out sideways and one plait unravelling itself. It was just *so* embarrassing. And I really didn't want Simon hearing about it.

A nice girl called Susha Patel had obviously felt sorry for me, 'cos she'd offered me the lend of one of her hairslides, so now I was back to being grand again, with both plaits on top of my head. Simon needn't ever have known about my bad hair day if Sam hadn't gone and blurted it out. I suppose she was only trying to be helpful. But when you're with someone as gorgeous and sophisticated as Simon, you really don't want to go into details of how disgusting yob-like boys have been pulling at your hair and going 'Ding dong'.

Sometimes I think Sam isn't very sensitive. But Simon was! He could see I didn't want to talk about it and so ever so quickly he changed the subject. He was what Mum would call dip-lo-mat-ic.

'Did you ever play the animals game?' he said.

'No,' I said, brightly. 'What's the animals game?'

'It tells you things about yourself. Want to have a go?'

'Mmm!'

'OK. Here's what you have to do. What's your favourite animal?'

'Um . . . dog.'

'What's your second favourite animal?'

'Cat!'

'And what's your third?'

I had to think about that one. 'Donkey?'

'Right. Now Sam!'

For a moment I thought she wasn't going to play, but then she said, 'Oh, all right! If I must. My favourite animal is a . . . crocodile!'

I said, 'Crocodile?'

'Yeah! Why not?'

'Ugh!' I screwed up my nose.

'It's her choice,' said Simon. 'What's your second?'

'A . . . panda!'

'Panda's all right,' I said. 'They're nice!'

'Third?'

'Oh, I dunno . . . elephant?'

'Elephants are nice, too,' I said.

'OK. So what's it all about?' demanded Sam.

'Tell you in a minute! Let's go and sit down.'

We all went to sit on the seat outside the sweet shop. The Radish squeezed in between me and Sam.

'Well, go on, then!' said Sam.

'First you've got to tell me *why* they're your favourites. Got a bit of paper?'

I opened my bag and tore a sheet out of my homework book.

'Right,' said Simon. 'Tell me what it is you like about them.'

I said that I liked dogs because they were funny and friendly and intelligent; and I liked cats because they were graceful and had minds of their own; and I liked donkeys because they were all niddy-noddy and gumpish.

A little smile turned up the corners of Simon's mouth.

'Niddy-noddy,' he said, writing it down. 'Sam? What about you?'

Sam, all defiant, said that she liked crocodiles because everyone was scared of them and they didn't have any enemies.

'Except man,' I said.

'A crocodile could eat a man,' said Sam, 'eat a man quite easy.'

I shuddered. Sam had very peculiar tastes!

'How about panda?' said Simon.

Still defiant, Sam said she liked pandas because they were all soft and cuddly, and she liked elephants because they were big and blundering and trampled on things.

'Well!' SImon looked at us, mischievously. 'Now

I'll tell you what it all means. Your first favourite is how you'd *like* to be.' He consulted his bit of paper. 'Abi would like to be funny and friendly and intelligent, and Sam would like everyone to be scared of her and not to have any enemies.'

There was a pause.

'Yeah, all right. Go on!' said Sam. 'What's the second one?'

'Second one is how you really are. Abi is graceful and has a mind of her own—'

Sam guffawed, and I blushed.

'What's so funny?' said Simon.

'She might have a mind of her own,' said Sam. 'But *graceful!*' She doubled over, clutching at her middle. It was unfortunate that as well as having had a bad hair day I'd also managed to trip over my own feet in a gym class and land upside down on the coconut matting. I'm not terribly good at gym. I couldn't blame Sam for laughing.

'Maybe she's graceful inside herself,' said Simon.

I liked the idea of that! 'What was Sam's second one?'

'Sam . . .' Simon looked down at his notes. 'Sam is soft and cuddly.'

This time there was a *long* pause. Then I giggled and Simon grinned and it was Sam's turn to go red.

'This is a rubbish game!' she said.

'Now we've started, we've got to finish.'

'Who says?'

'I do!' said Simon. 'Number three. This is how other people see you. Abi . . .' He stopped.

'Well? Get on with it!' said Sam.

Simon looked at me, apologetically. 'Niddy-noddy and gumpish.'

I swallowed.

'Niddy-noddy,' said the Radish; and he started wagging his head up and down. 'Niddy-noddy, niddy-noddy!'

I knew he wasn't laughing at me. He just liked the sound of the words.

'What was Sam? I said.

'Sam was . . . big and blundering and trampling on things.'

'Hah!' I said.

'Told you it was a rubbish game,' said Sam.

We left the seat and started off home.

'Let's ask the Radish,' I said; but the Radish said his favourite animal was an ant, 'cos it was creepy crawly, and his second favourite was a mouse, 'cos that was also creepy crawly, and his third favourite was a beetle–

' 'Cos *that's* creepy crawly!' Simon made creepy crawly movements with his fingers. The Radish clutched at me.

'What about you?' said Sam, looking at Simon.

'I can't play it! You can't play once you know what it's about. You'd cheat.'

'When you *did* play it.'

'When I did play it . . .' Simon crinkled his nose. He had a lovely nose. My stomach did a *blip* every time I looked at it.

'It's too long ago. I can't remember.'

'That's not fair!'

'Life isn't,' said Simon. 'Hey, Radish! Want a lift?'

The Radish shook his head. His hand crept into mine.

'Come on! I'll give you a piggy-back!'

'He doesn't *want* one,' said Sam. 'He wants to *walk*.'

Hastily, I explained that he was probably scared his friends might see him. I didn't want Simon to feel hurt. And I certainly didn't see why Sam had to be so rude. I thought perhaps it was because she was cross about the animal game. But I could have been cross, too! I mean, *niddy-noddy*. And gumpish! Sam had kept saying it was rubbish, but I wasn't so sure. Maybe people really did see me as a donkey! And I knew some people saw Sam as big and blundering. So maybe there was something in it?

I couldn't help wondering what Simon would have chosen. Something smooth and sleek . . . I spent the rest of the way home thinking of animals that were worthy of being compared to

Simon. I thought of: tiger, panther, jaguar, dolphin and horse. Racehorse, naturally! He could have been any one of those.

I asked Sam what she thought he might have chosen and she said. 'Rat, Dung beetle. Hyena.' Which was just stupid, so that I wished I hadn't asked her. She couldn't ever say anything nice about Simon.

After tea, I went upstairs to my bedroom. I wanted to be private and try out new hairstyles. Only Jack was allowed to come with me. We'd taken him for his walk, so he was quite tired and was happy just to lie on the bed and watch. Dad was still out plumbing, and Mum had gone next door to visit our neighbour Mrs Tizzard. (On the other side from Mrs Pink.)

Sam was up the road at Mary-Jo's. She didn't specially like Mary-Jo but they were both in the netball team and they wanted to put in some extra practice. Mary-Jo had her own netball and her dad had made her a proper hoop so she could practise shooting. Lissie Thomas was going round there, as well. I might have been a bit jealous once, but I wasn't any more. I knew we couldn't do *everything* together. And anyway, I had my garden! When I'd finished messing with my hair I was going to start making some little flowers to go in my thimble flower pots.

I glanced out of the window and saw Simon and the Radish, crouched together by the compost heap. Simon seemed to be showing the Radish something. That was good! The Radish was in a clinging mood. He'd tried to come upstairs with me but I'd told him quite firmly to go and watch telly. I didn't want *anyone* up there with me. Trying out new hairstyles is a very personal sort of thing.

Anyway. I decided in the end that I was going to wear it like I had that morning, plaited on top of my head, but this time I was going to stick some of Mum's hairpins in it. That way those horrible boys wouldn't be able to snatch at it, or pull it, or go 'Ding dong'.

'Hey! Abi!' Simon had seen me at the window.

He was waving at me. 'Come down, I've got something to show you!'

I hurried downstairs and into the garden. The Radish was still crouched by the compost heap.

'In here,' said Simon. 'Look!' He flung open the shed door. 'Ta-da, ta-da!'

'*Oh!*' I clasped my hands to my cheeks. 'You've done it!'

He had made the wooden frame for my garden. It had a little wall round three sides, and a little gate at the end, and a little archway, just like he'd promised. It even had its own little garden shed and a crazy-paving path.

'Do you like it?'

'It's *brilliant!*' I said.

'Look, I got you this, as well.' A little pink sunshade! 'I'll make a table and chairs next, and then I'll make a swing. All you've got to do is make some bushes and flowers.'

'I'll start straight away!' I said. 'I've already got the thimbles and some crinkly paper.'

'What I thought we could do with the *front*

garden,' said Simon, as we left the shed, 'we could have trees. I mean, made-up trees, but nice tall ones.'

'Yes, like fir trees or oak trees or—' I broke off. 'Radish,' I said, 'what are you doing?'

'We've been studying insects,' said Simon.

It didn't look to me as if the Radish was studying insects. It looked to me as if he was – chopping up worms!

'*Radish!*' I screeched. 'Stop that!'

The Radish sprang round, guiltily.

'What on earth do you think you're doing?' I said.

He looked at me, big-eyed. 'Cuttin' up wormth.'

'I can see that!' I said. 'But what are you doing it for?'

The Radish's eyes shifted furtively. His thumb went into his mouth.

'Radish,' said Simon. He squatted down beside him. Gently he said, 'Why were you doing it?'

The Radish sucked frantically on his thumb.

'Tell us,' said Simon. 'Tell us why you were doing it.'

'Wanted to thee what happenth.'

He whispered it so low I could hardly hear.

'You what?' I said.

'Wanted to see what happenth.'

'What do you *think* happens? What do you think would happen to you if someone chopped you in half? How can you be so cruel?'

It's not good to be cross with the Radish. He was already starting to cringe away and shake. But I couldn't have him being unkind to animals! Not even to humble worms.

'I thought you *liked* worms?' I said.

'Don't be angry with him,' begged Simon. He put his arm round the Radish's shoulder. 'Someone probably told him that you can chop worms in half and make two worms. He didn't mean to hurt them. Did you?'

The Radish shook his head. His thumb had gone back in his mouth. He'd stuffed it right the way in.

'Don't ever do it again!' I scolded. '*And where did you get that knife?*'

'That was my fault.' Simon said it quickly. He wasn't going to let the Radish take the blame. 'I was working in the shed. I must have left it lying about.'

'Well. All right. But you mustn't *do* things like that to living creatures!' I said.

It really upset me, the Radish chopping up worms. I told Mum about it and she said, 'I'm sure he didn't mean any harm. He's only a little boy! He was probably just experimenting.'

'Like when he tried to shoot Felix, I suppose!'

'I don't think he even realised what he was doing,' said Mum. 'He was so upset afterwards, poor little mite!'

'So he should have been.' I choked. 'Cutting up worms and shooting arrows at cats!'

'We'll keep an eye on him,' said Mum. 'It may be he's feeling a bit insecure, with another boy in the house. He might just be trying to assert himself. Lots of love and cuddles, that's what he needs! What he doesn't need—' Mum paused, to let it sink in. 'He doesn't need us being cross with him. That'll just make him even more insecure.'

I sort of understood what Mum was saying. All the same, I still felt upset.

5

That night I was happily lying in bed, all curled up with Jack underneath the duvet, when I opened my eyes to find a ghostly figure standing by the side of me. I nearly screamed! I am a bit scared of ghosts, to tell you the truth. Some people would give anything to see one, but not me! If anyone were ever to dress up in a sheet and go 'Oo hoo hoo' at me in the middle of the night I would most probably have a heart attack.

Anyway I quickly realised that it wasn't a ghost, 'cos Jack was wagging his stumpy tail under the duvet and making little excited squeaking noises, so I looked again and saw that it was the Radish. My heart sank.

'Oh, Radish!' I said. 'You haven't?'

He had! He'd wet the bed. His pyjamas were all sopping.

'Oh, *Radish*,' I said.

It was ages since he'd done that! We all thought he'd grown out of it. When he first came to us he'd done it every night, practically, 'cos he was such a sad little frightened person. He'd been so badly treated. It was a sign of insecurity, Mum said. But then, once he'd learnt that no one was going to be cross with him, and that he wasn't going to be sent away, he'd started going the whole night through without any accidents at all. He was ever so proud!

And now it had happened again.

'Radish,' I said, 'You're not feeling insecure, are you?'

The Radish just hiccuped, and trembled in his wet pyjamas.

'Let's get you cleaned up,' I said.

'Not tell anyone,' whispered the Radish.

I didn't say anything 'cos I felt that I would have to tell Mum. Not Sam or Dad or Simon, but Mum would have to know. Fortunately she'd left the rubber sheet on the bed, just in case; but I didn't see how we could get the bedclothes washed and dried without her noticing.

'Abi!' The Radish tugged at my hand as we tiptoed along the passage to the bathroom. 'Not tell!'

'Sh!' I said. I put a finger to my lips. 'You'll wake someone up.'

I fetched him some clean pyjamas and got him out of his dirty ones, then I sponged him down and wiped him dry and smuggled him back into my room and into bed with Jack, whose tail thumped so loudly I thought Mum and Dad would surely hear it in the next room. Jack's idea of heaven would be a bed full of bodies! Of course it is how dogs sleep when they are puppies, all in a great heap, cuddled together.

'You stay here,' I told the Radish. 'I'll go and put the sheet in the washing machine.'

'And not tell?'

'We'll keep it our secret,' I promised. The poor little Radish, he was so anxious! And I knew that Mum would never let on. 'You stay with Jack. I'll be back in a minute.'

I hauled the wet sheet off the bed, rolled the pyjamas into it, and staggered out with them into the hall. Just at that moment, the door of the spare room opened a crack and Simon's head peered out.

'Something wrong?' he said.

'Oh, um . . . no, it's nothing, it's all right, it's just—' I waved a hand and a loop of wet sheet went flobbing on to the floor. Quickly I gathered it up.

'Doing some washing?' said Simon.

'Oh! Yes! Ha!' I snickered brightly, as if washing bedclothes in the middle of the night was something really amusing. And then I became aware of a strong smell of piddle rising up, and I am ashamed to say that I panicked. 'It's the Radish,' I gabbled. 'He's had a bit of an accident.'

I know it was breaking my promise, but I didn't want him thinking *I'd* had the accident. I mean – well! I suppose I could have said that it was Jack. But I'm not very good in emergencies.

Sam is. But my brain just kind of seizes up.

'Poor little kid!' said Simon. 'Shall I come and help?'

We crept down to the kitchen. Simon was wearing green pyjamas. Gorgeous day-glo green, in some sort of shiny material. Dad's are boring stripes and the Radish's have little blue bunnies on them. Simon's were dead superior! I wished I'd put my dressing gown on, 'cos my nightie was all pink and little-girlish. Ugh! It made me cringe, thinking what I looked like in it.

'Does he do this often?' said Simon, as we programmed the washing machine and bundled all the wet stuff in there.

'Only when he's feeling insecure,' I said. 'He's been really good just lately.'

'I hope it isn't me,' said Simon.

'Why should it be you?' I said.

'Well! I guess he might feel threatened, or something.'

I nodded, gravely. 'We thought of that. But he's got to get used to it!. He knows that we love him and that we wouldn't ever send him away.'

'But does he?' said Simon.

'We've told him often enough!'

'People can change their minds though, can't they? You can't ever be really sure.'

I looked at him, doubtfully. 'I'm going to let him sleep with me and Jack for the rest of the night. He likes that.'

'I bet he does!' said Simon.

The way he said it made my heart go *BOING* all over again.

Before going back to bed, I put a clean sheet on the Radish's bed so that I could tuck him in there again next morning, before Mum came to wake us up. That way we could pretend that she knew nothing about it.

The Radish was still awake. He wanted to talk.

'I'm thorry about the wormth,' he whispered.

'Oh, Radish! That's all right,' I said. 'You weren't to know. Some people say you can cut them in half and then you'll have two and they don't feel any pain, but I wouldn't like to be cut in half, would you?'

Solemnly, the Radish shook his head.

'It'th bad,' he said, 'ithn't it?'

'It is,' I agreed. 'It's very bad.'

'Would it be bad to cut a cat'th whithkerth off?'

'Yes!' I said. 'Very *very* bad.'

'Would it hurt them?'

'I don't know if it would hurt them, but it would be very cruel.'

'But it wouldn't hurt them?'

'Maybe not. But they *need* their whiskers!'

'What do they need them for?'

'Well, they . . . they feel things with them. They're very sensitive. And now I think we ought to go to sleep,' I said.

Obediently the Radish curled up and closed his eyes. I was glad we'd talked about the worms. It was good to discuss these things.

I set my alarm clock for six, and as soon as it went off I shook the Radish awake and hustled him back into his own bed; and then when Mum came in, I told her what had happened.

'Oh, Abi, you are a good girl!' she said. 'That was really thoughtful of you.'

'Does it mean he's insecure?' I said.

Mum sighed. 'I suppose it probably does. Maybe it was a mistake after all, saying we'd take Simon.'

'Mum, no!' I said. I was terrified she might say that Simon had to go.

'I don't know.' Mum shook her head. 'I just felt . . . we're so lucky, living in a house like this! We have so much room. And there are so many children out there needing a home and someone to love them.'

'Well, this is it,' I said.

I knew how Mum felt. It's the way I feel about animals. I would love to go to a rescue centre and adopt hundreds of them! I would have a house full to bursting with cats and dogs. Mum would have a house full of children! But her next words made icy fingers clutch at my heart . . .

'Whatever happens,' she said, 'we can't have Gus upset.'

'You can't send Simon away!' I cried. 'He hasn't done anything! It wouldn't be fair!'

'We won't send Simon away. But we're all going to have to make a great effort to give little Gus his confidence back. We must all be extra-specially nice to him. Maybe Dad should take him out somewhere next Sunday, for a treat. Just Gus, on his own. Make him feel important. That's what we'll do! I'll have a word with him about it.'

Later that day, we took the dogs up the park. Simon came with us, which didn't please Sam but pleased me 'cos I hoped we might bump into Mary-Jo and Lissie and I might see Mary-Jo go weak at the knees again and Lissie's eyes come out on stalks. (Alas, it didn't happen!)

As we were walking up the road Simon said to the Radish, 'You mustn't let it worry you, you know. Having accidents, I mean. It happens to lots of us. It even happened to me! You'll grow out of it.'

I thought that was just so sweet of Simon! Saying that it had happened to him. I didn't expect it really had – I mean, not *Simon!* – but he didn't mind saying it, just to make a little boy feel better.

I'd forgotten the Radish hadn't wanted anyone to know. His hand urgently tugged at mine. I looked down at him. His face was all crumpled and crimson. Too late, I remembered! I'd promised not to tell. And now not only Simon knew about it, but Sam, as well. Oh, dear! I did feel terrible. It was all my fault. I shouldn't ever have told Simon in the first place. But once I *had* told him, I should have sworn him to utmost secrecy.

'Radish, I'm sorry,' I whispered.

I wondered if he would ever forgive me.

'What was all that about?' demanded Sam, later, when we were on our own.

I told her what had happened and she curled her lip and said, 'Trust him!' She meant Simon, not the Radish. 'He would go and blab it, wouldn't he?'

'He didn't know,' I said. 'I should have told him.'

'Well, but fancy *talking* about it. In front of people! That's really sensitive, that is.'

'Just like you are,' I said.

Sam's hands flew to her hips. 'What d'you mean, just like I am?'

'*Big and blundering.*'

She didn't like that. 'I told you,' she said, 'that game was rubbish!'

I had to work really hard to get the Radish to forgive me. I went to see him after he'd gone to bed. I sat on the edge of his bed and read one of his favourite stories to him, something called *Gussy the Pop-Eyed Whopping Dog*, which he knows practically by heart. After I'd read it, I said, 'Radish, I'm really really really sorry about telling Simon. I didn't mean to! But he saw me carrying the sheet downstairs and he . . . well, he guessed.' I couldn't quite bring myself to admit that I'd got in a panic in case he thought it was mine. 'So I'm *truly* sorry and please will you forgive me?

88

'Cos I do love you ever so much!'

The Radish is such a dear sweet little boy! He doesn't bear grudges, any more than Felix. He threw his arms round my neck and kissed me and said, 'I forgive you, Abi!' And then he whispered, 'Can I come an' thleep wiv you again?'

'Well . . .' I hesitated. It was OK him coming to sleep with me *after* he'd had an accident, but I didn't have a rubber sheet on my bed!

'Pleethe, Abi! *Pleethe!*' He was clinging with both arms round my neck. How could I refuse him?

'OK,' I said. 'But you'll have to wait till Mum and Dad are in bed. I'll come and get you!'

I set my trusty alarm clock for midnight, and I put it under my pillow so that no one would hear it except me; then when it went off, I crept in and woke the Radish and brought him back to my room and we all slept soundly right round till morning. And the bed was dry as a bone! It seemed he didn't have accidents when he slept with me and Jack.

After that, he wanted to sleep with me every night. I wasn't quite sure that Mum would approve – I mean, she might say it was making him too dependent, or something – but after all, we were supposed to be being extra-specially nice to him. Mum had said! So I didn't really see how she could complain. Apart from anything else, it was saving her a whole load of washing. She ought to be grateful!

Me, I just wanted the Radish to feel happy and secure. Partly because it upset me to think he might be *un*happy, and partly I desperately didn't want Mum deciding that fostering Simon had been a mistake. I didn't think I could bear it if she were to ask Miss Davies to take him back. I'd got used to him being there! It was like having an older brother. A *polite* older brother. An older brother who didn't jeer at you for doing girls' things or pull your hair and go 'Ding dong!' I was really going to miss him when he started back at school in a week's time.

On Tuesday, Lissie Thomas went round handing out invitation cards for her birthday party. I got one and so did Sam. So did Mary-Jo, natch. So did Susha Patel and a quiet girl called Bethany Proctor. Lauren Babcock and Alison Peach didn't. Nor did Jasmine Potter.

'I don't invite just *any*body,' said Lissie. She made it sound like she was doing us this huge immense favour, which, in a way I suppose she was. She and Mary-Jo were the two most popular girls in the class. I don't know why; they just were. So naturally everyone wanted to go to their parties.

'Aren't you having any boys?' said Sam.

'Yes, but only a few. A few special ones. Like my cousin and Mary-Jo's brother and a friend of his. Simon can come, if he likes.' Her cheeks went all blushy when she said this. 'Do you think he'd like to?'

'Shouldn't think so,' said Sam.

'He might,' I said.

Lissie looked at me, eagerly. 'Shall I give you an invitation for him?'

She'd already written one out!

'We don't want him coming,' grumbled Sam, as we went home after school.

'Why not?'

''Cos he's smarmy!'

'I s'pose you'd rather have a bonehead like Charlie Potts!'

'At least he doesn't *smarm*.'

'Oh, shut up!' I said. 'What are you going to wear?'

'Who knows?' said Sam. 'Who cares? Clothes don't interest me. I'll probably wear a dustbin bag!'

Sometimes Sam is just *impossible*.

On Sunday, after we'd walked the dogs, me and Sam went into town together, to the shopping centre. We were going to do a bit of mooching and see if we could find anything to wear to the party. Well, I was going to see if I could find anything to wear. Sam kept saying that clothes didn't interest her, which I knew for a fact wasn't true. She was into trainers in a big way. She had *three pairs*, all expensive. Plus she had this black jacket she really liked 'cos it made her look cool, and a pair of black jeans that went with it. So it wasn't true that clothes didn't interest her. She was just saying it to make me feel like a bimbo.

Actually she was saying it because of Simon.

'You only want to dress up to try and impress *him!*'

Sometimes I think that girls can be just as horrid as boys. They are simply horrid in a different kind of way.

When we got back the house was empty, except for Jack and Daisy. Dad had gone up to town with the Radish, to a model railway exhibition. It was the treat Mum had promised him, to make him feel special. I don't think he was terribly interested in model railways, but he'd been dead excited at the thought of going up to town all by himself with Dad! Me and Sam kept saying, 'Oh, you're so lucky! I wish we could come!' But Dad had said, 'Sorry, girls! This is strictly for us.' And the Radish had pummelled his cheeks and said, 'Thorry, girlth! Thith ith thrictly for uth!'

Mum had left us a note on the kitchen table: *Next door with Mrs T. Ring if you need me.*

Sam pulled a face. Mum was always having to drop in next door to see Mrs Tizzard. Sam and me called her 'Mrs Tizzy' 'cos she got in such terrible tizzes. Mum said that when we were her age we would get in tizzes.

'She's very old. She's over eighty. Someone has to keep an eye on her.'

'Wonder what it is this time?' said Sam. 'Men in stocking masks swarming up the drainpipe?'

I started to giggle, and then reminded myself that Mrs Tizzard was over eighty.

'I wonder where Simon is?'

'Dunno,' said Sam. 'Don't care, either!'

I looked in the garden and in the shed, but he wasn't there. Then I knocked on his bedroom door and called 'Simon!' but he wasn't there, either. He still wasn't there when Mum got back from Mrs Tizzy's.

'Was it men swarming up the drainpipe?' said Sam.

'No, it was her cats,' said Mum.

Mrs Tizzard had two sweet cats: Peony and Polo, both quite ancient. Sometimes when Felix wasn't about they came and sunned themselves on our wall.

'Has something happened to them?' I said.

'Yes, it's rather worrying. They've both—' Mum hesitated.

'Both what?' I said.

'They've both had chunks of fur hacked off them. They haven't actually been hurt, but . . . well! She's very upset. Obviously.'

'Mum, that's horrible!' I said.

'Yes, it is. I've told her to keep them in for the next few days. Where's Felix, by the way?'

'Felix!' My hand flew to my mouth. Where was he? He usually came to greet us when we got in.

Sam dashed out into the garden, calling his name. Mum and I searched the house. I was the one who found him – fast asleep on the Radish's bed! It was a huge relief.

'Do you think we ought to keep him in, as well?' said Sam.

'We could try,' said Mum.

But Felix isn't used to being kept in, and he was a whole lot younger than Peony and Polo.

'We'll keep him in for the rest of the day,' said Mum, 'and then he'll have to take his chance. It was probably just some stupid child. They won't do it again.'

In all the worry over Felix, I'd almost forgotten about Simon. Then I remembered and asked Mum where he was, and she said he'd been restless and decided to go out.

'I think he's a bit bothered about having to go back to school tomorrow. I don't think he gets on with the other boys too well.'

Sam gave a little snort, which she hastily

turned into a cough when me and Mum looked at her.

'He has to play rugby,' I said. 'It's even worse than ordinary football.'

'Boo hoo!' said Sam.

Sam, of course, would just love to play rugby.

It was three o'clock when Simon arrived back. He turned up with Dad and the Radish. He'd been there, at the station, when they got in from London.

'I hope you weren't thinking of running away!' said Mum. I had the feeling she was only half joking and I turned to Simon in alarm. Why would he run away??? But very solemnly he said that he had been watching the trains.

'He's an anorak!' hissed Sam at me, later on, in delight. 'An old anoraky train watcher!'

That night we made sure Felix was safely locked in. We didn't want any hateful person chopping bits of *his* fur off. Felix is pure white and Dad is always saying – in fun, of course – that he would make a lovely pair of gloves.

When I crept in to fetch the Radish and take him back to my bed I found Felix crouched at the top of the stairs. He miaowed at me most piteously so I let him come in, as well, and he settled down as good as gold on top of the duvet.

'Radish,' I said. There was something nagging at me, and I had to ask him. 'Radish . . . you didn't cut any fur off Mrs Tizzy's cats, did you?'

The Radish looked at me, his eyes all owly.

'Someone chopped some of their fur off. It wasn't you, was it?'

'Not me, not me!' The Radish shook his head, vigorously. 'It wathn't me! I didn't do it!'

'All right,' I said. 'I'm sorry.'

'I didn't, I didn't! It wathn't me!'

The Radish was growing really agitated. He was tossing from side to side and banging his head on the pillow.

'It wathn't, it wathn't, it—'

'Radish, I believe you!' I said. 'It's all right, I believe you!'

I turned the light out and put my arms round him and cuddled him close to me, trying to stop him shaking. I almost wished I hadn't asked him, but it had been going round my head all night.

'Go to sleep,' I whispered.

That night, the Radish wet the bed.

My bed.

6

On Monday, Simon started back at school. I could tell he didn't want to go. He was all quiet and subdued, so that I felt really sorry for him. I would hate to go to boarding school! I know in books it always sounds fun, what with midnight feasts and cream teas when your mum and dad come to visit, but I couldn't bear to be separated from Jack!

Simon said, 'I'm really going to miss you. Even the animals!' So I knew he felt the same way.

'It's only for a few days,' said Mum, all bright and cheerful. 'You'll be back here before you know it!'

I sometimes think Mum lives on a different time scale from the rest of us. She, for instance, is always complaining that time *gallops*. I don't find that it does! Except perhaps sometimes, when I'm having fun. Other times, it positively s..n..a..i..l..s. Even just a lesson that you don't happen to like, such as in my case netball ('cos of people like Sam and Mary-Jo yelling at me all the time . . . *Pass, Abi, pass! Oh, you IDIOT!*) even a 40-minute lesson can seem to last for ever. Five days was practically a life sentence.

'I'll finish the garden while you're away,' I promised. I thought it would be something for him to look forward to. 'Oh, and there's the party! Don't forget the party!'

To Sam's disgust, Simon had accepted Lissie's invitation. The party was on Saturday, and I was feeling quite excited by it, specially now that Simon was coming!

'What do you want for dinner on Friday night?' said Mum. 'You choose!'

She was obviously trying to give him something to look forward to, as well. Simon glanced across at me and grinned.

'Burgers and chips,' he said.

Hurray! He knew that was my favourite!

It seemed strange, walking back from school

that afternoon without Simon. Just me and Sam and the Radish, like it always used to be. When poor old Ellen had been with us we used to get so mad at her, always hanging round after us. But I'd really waited for that moment when we came out of the school gates and saw Simon standing there with the Radish. I'd enjoyed the looks on people's faces. *And* the way Gary Copestake and Charlie Potts didn't give us any hassle. Simon was bigger than them and stronger than them. They wouldn't have dared!

'Can you imagine,' I said to Sam, 'what it would be like, going to boarding school?'

'I wouldn't mind,' said Sam.

'You wouldn't?' I stared at her, hurt.

'Well, not so long as we were both there,' said Sam. 'It'd be fun!'

'What about Jack and Daisy?'

'Oh! Yeah. Well . . .' She obviously hadn't thought about Jack and Daisy.

'They'd hate it!' I said.

Sam brightened. 'Some schools let you take your animals with you.'

'I bet Simon's doesn't. *And* he has to play rugby!'

'Not this term, dummy. This term's tennis.' Sam tossed an imaginary ball high into the air and brought her right arm down, *SMASH!* on top of it. Well, actually she brought it down with a smash on top of my shoulder. 'Ow! That hurt!' I said.

'Sorry,' said Sam. 'But it was an ace serve! That's ten-love to me. I wonder if old Soppy Simon plays tennis?'

'He's not soppy,' I said, rubbing my shoulder.

'Smarmy. Smarmy Simon!'

Usually when one of us makes up a nickname – like the Radish, or Droopy Drawers – we both latch on to it. We go round giggling about it, and repeating it over and over. But I just didn't think that Smarmy Simon was funny. He wasn't smarmy!

I said this, indignantly, to Sam.

'Yes, he is,' she said. 'He's smarmy as can be! You've just got a thing about him.'

My cheeks did a fast burn. Like one minute they were their normal pasty white, the next a scorching bubble of hot tomato. Sizzle sizzle, bright red.

'See?' crowed Sam. 'You're blushing!' She turned triumphantly to the Radish. 'Abi's got a thing about Smarmy Simon!'

'You horrible scumbag!' I shrieked. 'I haven't!'

'Yes, you have! You've got a thing about him!'

She went on chanting it all up the road. 'Abi's got a thing about Smarmy Simon!' She even got the Radish going.

'Thmarmy Thimon, Thmarmy Thimon! Abi'th got a thing about Thmarmy Thimon!'

At times like that, I almost begin to think that being an Only did have some advantages.

That night, and the following night, and the night after that, and the night after that, the Radish stayed in his own bed right through till morning without any accidents at all. Brilliant!

But on Friday Simon was home again, and guess what? The Radish was back! He came creeping into my bed at half-past twelve and I didn't have the heart to turn him out. It seemed that Mum was right. Simon being there was making him feel insecure.

I tried to talk to him about it. I told him there wasn't any need. To feel insecure, I mean.

'We love you, Radish! You're one of the family! Simon isn't. He's just a foster. One day soon – they'll probably find his dad and then he'll go and live with him. But you're not going anywhere! You're staying with us.'

'Thtay *here*.' The Radish curled up, with his arms round my neck. 'Thtay here wiv you!'

It wasn't very comfortable, spending the night with the Radish's arms locked round my neck, but I didn't like to move in case he thought I didn't want him and got even more insecure. They were only weedy little arms, but I still woke up with a crick.

Next day was Saturday. The day of the party.

'What are you going to wear?' I asked Sam.

'Told you,' she said. 'A dustbin bag!'

She didn't, of course. (Though I wouldn't put it past her! I wouldn't put anything past Sam). When it actually came to it, she arrived downstairs in her black jeans with a black T-shirt and her black jacket. Mum took one look and shrieked, 'Sam, you're going to a party, not a funeral! You're far too young to wear black!'

'It isn't *all* black,' said Sam. And it was true. She was also wearing some sparkly bangles I'd once given her and a gold chain with the letter S, which had been one of her Christmas presents. I had to admit, she looked dead cool! I couldn't help feeling a bit envious and wishing that I'd dressed in black, too. Except that I couldn't, 'cos I didn't have any black in my wardrobe. Well, apart from my new slinky tights, which I was wearing with one of my new short skirts – blue – with a pink top and red jacket.

Mum approved of what I was wearing.

'That's nice,' she said. 'That's pretty! That's what a young girl *should* wear.'

Which immediately plunged me into gloom, 'cos who wants their mum to approve?

It's odd, now I stop to think about it. When it came to decorating my dolls' house it was Sam who insisted on all the bright colours and me who wanted to be tasteful. When it came to buying clothes, we were exactly the other way round! I was the one who chose red things and blue things and mixed them all together. Maybe, I thought sadly, I didn't have any dress sense. I could dress rooms; but I couldn't dress me!

But at least I'd solved the problem of my hair. I'd pulled it back in a pony tail and fixed it with a blue butterfly hairclip I'd bought last week when me and Sam had gone into the shopping centre. I couldn't have worn it like that at school because of Gary Copestake and Charlie Potts. A pony tail! It would be asking for trouble. But I knew there wouldn't be any boys like that at Lissie's party. She'd told us, there were only going to be *nice* boys. Her cousin and Mary-Jo's brother and Mary-Jo's brother's friend. And, of course, Simon!

'Enjoy yourselves,' said Mum, as she dropped us off at Lissie's. 'I'll see you later.'

Lissie's party was way, way the best party I had ever been to. It wasn't like an ordinary party. Lissie's mum ran a riding school, and the party was held in a field next to the stable. There was a big stripy tent with long tables all laid out with delicious yummy food which you could just go and help yourself to whenever you felt like it. Lissie's dad came with a video camera and made a video of us, which we all got to watch before we went home. Then her mum saddled some of the horses and brought them into the field and people like Lissie and Mary-Jo, who had both learnt to ride, showed off for a bit by galloping round and jumping over things such as wooden gates and piles of old car tyres, until Mrs Thomas said it was time other people had a go.

Sam was the first to scramble up. She couldn't wait! But after walking round the field all sedately with Lissie's mum leading her, she then boastfully declared that she could manage on her own. So Lissie's mum gave her a hard hat to wear and off she went, all by herself.

'Just walk!' cried Lissie's mum; but walking isn't Sam's idea of fun, and it obviously wasn't the horse's idea, either, 'cos before we knew it they were going round at a simply tremendous rate, with Sam slipping sideways in the saddle and clinging like mad to the bit that sticks up. The pommel, I think it's called. Of course, she fell off. And of course, she jumped straight back up again! I sometimes think that Sam isn't scared of anything.

By the end of the afternoon she was doing what Lissie called 'rising to the trot', which apparently means going up and down at the same time as the horse instead of bouncing about like a pea in a bucket, which is what most beginners do. It looked most uncomfortable to me, but Sam said it was brilliant and she was going to ask Mum if she could have lessons.

'You should,' Lissie told her. 'You're a natural!' She didn't even seem to mind that her beautiful black jeans were all covered in horsey hairs and grass stains. *She was a natural!*

I wasn't. I love horses like I love all animals; but I am a bit nervous of them, to tell you the truth. When you're sitting on top of one, it seems an awfully long way to the ground! Mary-Jo kept saying, 'Oh, come on, Abi! There's nothing to be frightened of.'

'You're not frightened of *dogs*,' said Lissie. 'And dogs can bite!'

'So can horses,' muttered Simon.

They do have rather big teeth, though it wasn't the teeth I was scared of! It was such a relief when Simon said very firmly but politely that he didn't ride. I was able to say that I didn't, either.

'Much safer down on the ground,' said Simon; and then he told me that he'd once had a very bad experience with a horse.

'Did it bite you?' I said.

'No, it kicked me. It was really vicious.'

Lissie overheard us. She said, 'Horses aren't vicious!'

'This one was,' said Simon.

'In that case, you must have done something to it,' said Lissie.

I thought that was so unfair! She was almost making like it was Simon's fault. I felt sorry for Simon, sometimes. He was one of those people that animals just don't get on with. No matter how hard he tried with Jack and Daisy, they wouldn't have anything to do with him. Felix wouldn't, either, but cats are peculiar. They are very picky. Dogs are usually eager to be friends with anyone.

'I can't stand horsey people,' said Simon.

'No,' I said, 'especially if they hunt. I think it's really cruel, chasing foxes. Don't you?'

'Absolutely,' said Simon.

I was so glad we agreed!

After the horsey people had stopped being horsey, and the horses – or ponies, actually, according to Lissie – had been put back in their boxes, Mary-Jo's brother's friend, who was called Anthony, set up this disco he'd got and we had dancing. Me and Simon danced together! It didn't seem to matter that I couldn't dance. I mean, I'd always thought I'd be too embarrassed, being the sort of person that trips over her own feet in gym class, but Simon said there was nothing to it.

'You just jig about to the music.' And then he said, 'If you're not going to dance then I'm not, either. I don't feel like doing it with any of those other gawkers.

I giggled and said, 'What's gawkers?'

'Dweebs and horsey people,' said Simon.

Well I didn't think that *everyone* was a dweeb. Susha Patel wasn't, for instance; she was really nice. And Beth Proctor, too. They weren't horsey people, either. On the other hand, I couldn't help feeling flattered. I was the only one Simon would dance with!

'What about Sam?' I said. I forced myself to say it. I didn't want to be disloyal to her. 'Wouldn't you like to dance with Sam?'

But Simon shuddered and said Sam was one of the *last* people he'd like to dance with. I couldn't really blame him. Sam had been horrible to him from the word go.

Mum came to fetch us at eight o'clock.

'Did you have a good time?' she said. 'What did you do? Did you play games?'

There was a pause.

'What sort of . . . games?' said Sam.

'Oh! I don't know. Blind Man's Buff, Postman's Knock—'

'Musical Chairs?' said Simon.

'Yes!' Mum beamed. 'Musical Chairs!'

'*Mum,*' I said.

'What?' said Mum. 'What have I done now?'

'That sort of stuff's for babies,' I said.

'Is it?' Mum seemed surprised. 'It's what I used to play at your age.'

It's what we'd played at my last party, too. But that was ages ago. I'd grown up since then!

'So what did you do,' said Mum, 'if you didn't play games?'

'We rode horses,' said Sam. 'Lissie said I was a natural! I was wondering . . . do you think I could have lessons?'

'Instead of gym classes?' said Mum.

'Yeah! Well . . .' Sam hesitated. She was really good at gym. She was hoping to be picked for the local under-12s. 'Dunno about *instead*.'

'One or the other,' said Mum, firmly. 'We couldn't run to both. How about Abi? Does she want to learn, too?'

'Not me,' I said. 'I'm not a horsey person!'

That night when I went to bed, I was still fizzing and zinging with excitement. I kept reliving all the things that had happened at the party. Mainly the dancing. I still couldn't get over it . . . me, dancing! Me, with Simon! He obviously didn't think I was stupid and babyish in spite of my blue skirt and my pink top, which Mum said was *pretty*.

It took me ages to get to sleep. Ages and ages. I heard the clock downstairs striking the hours and the half hours and I began to despair. I hate lying awake when everyone else is asleep! You feel like you're all alone in the house, which in a way you are. It's really spooky!

In the end I must have gone to sleep, 'cos if I hadn't gone to sleep the Radish wouldn't have been able to wake me up. I felt something dabbing at me, and I opened an eye, all bleary and blurred, to see this white shape hovering by the side of the bed. I groaned.

'*Radish*,' I said. 'What's the matter now?'

I expect I probably sounded a bit irritable.

'Just go back to your own bed,' I said. 'You can't keep coming in here all the time!' And I hauled the duvet up to my chin and clutched at it with both hands. The Radish was seven years old! It was time he learnt. He'd have to stand on his own feet sooner or later.

For a few seconds he went on hovering. Determinedly, I screwed my eyes tight shut.

'Just go away,' I muttered.

When I finally risked a peek over the top of the duvet, he had disappeared. And of course I immediately felt like the meanest person on earth. How could I be so unkind? To the poor little Radish, of all people!

I tossed and I turned and I thumped the pillow into weird shapes but it still felt like a lump of lead and I just knew that no way was I ever going to get back to sleep again. With a sigh, I slid out of bed and pattered along the landing to the Radish's room.

'Radish?' I whispered.

He wasn't there. Neither was his sheet. He had obviously had an accident and come to me for comfort. And I had turned him away! He must have dragged the sheet off the bed and hauled it down to the kitchen to wash. I thought I'd heard strange slithery sounds and creaks on the stairs. I'd tried to pretend it wasn't happening 'cos I really hadn't wanted to get out of bed! But now that I was out, I couldn't leave that poor little boy to manage all by myself. I would have to go down and make sure he was all right.

7

I sneaked down the stairs as quietly as I could and along the hall to the kitchen. As I opened the kitchen door, there was a blood-curdling wail and Felix sprang at me. I very nearly screamed! It's quite frightening when a cat launches itself at you out of nowhere. Plus he landed on my shoulder, which was – *OW! OUCH!* – really painful. I could feel his claws digging into me as he steadied himself. Felix *never* uses his claws; not unless he's absolutely terrified. He's a bit standoffish at times, but he's never mean. But those claws were like red-hot needles going in! I reached up to grab him, but I wasn't quite quick enough. Before I could get a proper hold he was off, tearing past me and up the hall as if a pack of wild dogs were after him.

And then I saw that Simon was in the kitchen as well as the Radish. The Radish was crouched on the floor by the washing machine. Simon was standing nearby. There was a great red gash down his cheek.

'What happened?' I whispered.

Simon pulled a face. 'I thought I heard a noise, so I came to investigate. It was Gus.' We both looked down at the little crouched figure. 'He's had a bit of an accident. I guess he was putting his sheet in the washing machine and . . .'

And what?

'The door must have been left open. Felix must have . . . I don't know! Decided to go to sleep in there. I hoicked him out, but—'

'He scratched you!'

'He was frightened.'

'You'd better put something on it,' I said. 'There's some stuff in the bathroom. Tea tree lotion. That's what Mum always uses.'

'I'll go and do it. And I'll take Gus back up and get him settled.'

'OK. I'll see to the sheet,' I said.

Simon held out a hand. 'Come on, then!' he

said. 'Let's get you back to bed.'

Obediently, the Radish allowed himself to be led from the kitchen. It was like he was in some kind of trance. He was wearing the top half of his blue bunny pyjamas – the bottom half was in with the wet sheet – and he looked so pathetic!

I turned to the washing machine. It was on the right setting; all I had to do was press the start button. I was really puzzled how Felix could have got in there. We are always most careful to check the door is properly closed. And even if it hadn't been, I didn't see how the Radish could have missed a big white furry cat curled up inside it.

I switched on to short wash and fetched myself some biscuits and a glass of milk while I settled down to wait. I had this idea that if I hung the sheet and the pyjama bottoms in the garden, they would be dry by morning; and then, if I set my alarm for really early, I could creep down and get them in and Mum need never know. I was just so scared that she was going to say

Simon would have to be sent away!

Simon came back down while I was still waiting, so I poured him a glass of milk as well and we sat there together, at the kitchen table, talking in low voices so as not to wake Mum or Dad.

'What was the Radish *doing?*' I whispered.

'Just trying to wash his sheet.'

'But surely he must have seen Felix in there?'

'Well . . . you'd have thought so,' said Simon. 'But maybe not if he just opened the door and started shoving stuff in.'

'It's very odd,' I said. 'I still don't see how it can have happened.'

Simon explained to me how he had come in just as the Radish was about to press the start button. To his horror he had seen Felix looking out at him through the glass panel of the door and had pressed the stop button just in time to snatch him out – which was when Felix, in his panic, had scratched his face and sprang yowling across the room to land on my shoulder.

'It wasn't his fault.'

'No, but your face is going to be ever such a mess,' I said.

'Doesn't matter. Why are we sitting down here, by the way? Are we waiting for something?'

'Waiting for the sheet to finish.'

I explained my plan for hanging it out to dry and getting it back in again before Mum could see it. What I didn't explain was the reason for my plan. I mean, I didn't want Simon feeling that he was under some kind of threat. But anyway, it all went for nothing 'cos even before we'd reached the final spin the kitchen door had opened and Mum had appeared.

'I thought so!' she said. 'Has he had another accident?'

'Yes, but we're seeing to it,' I told her.

'Oh, Abi, you didn't have to wash the sheet in the middle of the night!' Mum stepped forward and switched the machine off. 'It can wait till morning. Did I hear Felix, by the way?' And then she caught sight of Simon's face and said, 'How did that happen?'

'He's put stuff on it,' I said.

'But how did it happen?'

'He was getting Felix out of the washing machine.'

'Getting Felix out of the washing machine? What was he doing in the washing machine?'

'We don't know,' I said.

Simon explained all over again about finding Felix in the machine and Gus about to press the start button.

'Thank goodness you came down!' said Mum. 'I can't imagine how on earth he got in there. Poor little Gus! He must have been half asleep. Where is he now?'

Simon said that he had put him back to bed.

'And what about Felix? Where's he?'

'He ran into the house,' I said. 'I'll go and have a look for him. He's had a nasty shock.'

I found Felix hiding under the big chest on the upstairs landing. He wouldn't come out, no matter how hard I coaxed.

'Leave him,' said Mum. 'He'll come when he's ready.'

'But I want to cuddle him!'

'Shh! You'll wake Sam.'

Too late! I already had. She came tumbling out on to the landing with Daisy, wanting to know if the house was on fire.

'All I hear is people crashing about!'

So then of course I had to explain everything to her. Sam said, 'Oh, poor, poor Felix!' and we both plonked down flat on our stomachs to try and entice him out.

Felix still wouldn't come, and Dad slept through everything!

I didn't sleep at all. I couldn't; not after all that had happened. I kept thinking . . . suppose Simon hadn't gone downstairs when he did? Felix would have been drowned! Every time I closed my eyes I saw his round, white, furry face looking out at me through the glass panel of the washing machine door. Next morning, Sam confessed that exactly the same thing had happened to her.

'I had nightmares!'

'And who left the door open?' I said.

It could only have been Mum. I mean she's the only one, normally, that uses the washing machine. But it was Mum who told us originally that we must always, always take care to make sure the door was properly shut!

'I can only assume,' she said, 'that it sprang open. Either that or Felix jumped in while Gus wasn't looking.'

We couldn't ask the Radish. He was already quite upset enough, what with wetting the bed and then nearly drowning Felix. Mum said we weren't to badger him.

'It was just one of those things. Accidents will happen, no matter how you try to guard against them. Fortunately it had a happy ending, so don't get on poor little Gus's case.'

'I'm just a bit concerned,' said Dad, who was the only one to have had a good night's sleep (I reckon my dad could sleep through an earthquake). 'It worries me that he's started on this bed-wetting again.'

'He'll get over it,' I said, quickly.

'But why is he doing it? Are we putting him under too much stress?'

'Dad, he's got to learn!' I said.

'He's *seven years old*,' said Sam. 'He's too young to learn.'

'He's not! Don't be so ageist! He's not a baby.'

'But look at him.' Dad nodded out of the window. Simon had taken the Radish into the garden to search for bugs. We had one of those special bug boxes with a magnifying glass on top. Of course you always had to put the bugs back again when you'd finished studying them.

'That's not my idea of a carefree little boy,' said Dad.

I had to admit, I hadn't seen the Radish do any of his cheek-pummelling or hair-twizzling in ages. These are two of the things that he does when he's happy. When he's unhappy or frightened, he sucks his thumb and hunches his shoulders and sort of cringes into himself. Which was what he was doing now, out in the garden with Simon. Simon was trying to show him something in the bug box and the Radish was thumb-sucking like crazy and cowering into the bushes.

'It's not fair!' I cried. 'Simon tries so hard!'

'What's not fair?' said Mum.

'Blaming Simon!'

'No one's blaming him, Abi.'

'Yes, you are! You're saying it's because of him being here the Radish has gone all pathetic again.'

'Well, it is,' said Sam.

'You see? You're doing it! You're blaming him!'

'Abi, we are not.' Mum said it very firmly. 'Just put that idea right out of your head. We are not blaming Simon. If anyone's to blame, it's the person who abused Gus before he came to us. What we have to do is find a way of convincing him he's loved and wanted.'

'We've been doing that all week,' I muttered.

'Yes, that's true, and you've been a very good girl, letting him climb into bed with you.'

So she *knew*! And hadn't said anything! Trust Mum.

'But I think perhaps at weekends, while Simon's here, we've all got to make an extra-special effort. How about, for instance, if this afternoon the four of us – you, me, Sam, Gus – all went off for a picnic with the dogs, while your dad took Simon to the cricket? If it was just the four of us it might make him feel more secure.'

I didn't think I liked that idea very much.

'Wouldn't the Radish rather go and see the cricket?'

'He's too young! He couldn't sit there all that time.'

'Sam could,' I said. 'Sam and Dad could go to the cricket and the rest of us could have the picnic.'

'What's the point of that?' said Sam, witheringly.

'You like cricket!'

'But we're supposed to be doing things with the Radish. I s'ppose you'd rather do them with Smarmy Simon!'

'For heaven's sake, you two!' Mum said it impatiently. 'What's the matter with you both?'

'She's got a thing about Smarmy Simon!'

'Shut up! I have not!'

'Yes, you have! You've got a thing about him!'

'I have—'

'Sam and Abi, will you please stop this? We've got enough on our hands with Gus, without you two starting! Just make up your mind, Abi! Are you coming to the picnic or not?'

'*Me?*'

'Yes, you! You seem to be the one that's making all the fuss.'

'In that case—' I tossed my head. My nice new pony tail gave a satisfying *swish*. 'I'll go to the cricket.'

Sam's mouth gaped open. 'You hate cricket!'

'I'm sacrificing myself,' I said. 'I don't want Simon to feel he's being punished.'

'Punished?' Dad sounded hurt. 'Being taken to a cricket match? Most young lads would think that was a treat!'

'Simon's not like other boys,' I said. 'He's not into sports.'

Dad shook his head in disbelief.

'Of course, it's not like it's a first-class game,' said Sam. I think she only said it to reassure herself that she wasn't missing out. 'It's only amateurs.'

'They field a good team,' said Dad.

I didn't know whether they fielded a good team or not. I find cricket a total dead bore, to tell you the truth. Nothing ever seems to happen. At least in football people charge up and down and barge into each other and fall over in the mud and roll around clutching at themselves and writhing as if in agony. They don't do that in cricket. It's like a sort of still-life.

'Which side is which?' whispered Simon, after we'd been there about twenty minutes.

'Dunno,' I said. And then I added, 'Does it matter?'

'I want to know when to cheer and when to boo,' said Simon.

'I don't even understand the rules,' I said.

Simon spent the afternoon trying to explain them to me. He told me all about overs and hat tricks and no-balls. He told me about the different positions, such as cover point and third man and silly mid-on. I giggled at silly mid-on, and so did Simon. We did quite a lot of giggling. Dad kept shaking his head. He takes his cricket very seriously, does Dad. The best bit of the afternoon was when someone's dog got loose and went running on to the field and attacked one of the stumps. Me and Simon cheered at that. Dad just sucked in his breath.

The match wasn't going to finish till goodness knows what time, seven o'clock or something, but to my relief, at half-past five, Dad said that perhaps we'd better be going.

'Unless, of course,' he said hopefully, 'you'd rather stay?'

Me and Simon didn't dare to look at each other.

'Better not,' I said. 'I think Mum would probably like us home.'

'But thank you very much for bringing us,' said Simon, politely.

'Humph!' said Dad.

'No, really, I enjoyed it. Cricket's the only game I can bear to watch.'

He said it so earnestly that he almost managed to convince *me*! I think Dad was convinced. He said, 'Good! In that case we'll come again.'

'Did you *really* enjoy it?' I hissed, as we followed Dad back to the car.

'Only because you were there,' said Simon. (*Blush, blush, hot tomato.*) 'Actually, I think I'm some sort of freak . . . I'm not really into sports.'

'Nor me,' I said. Think of *coooooooool* water. Think of ice bergs. Think of *snow.* 'I s'ppose that makes me a freak, too.'

'It's all right for you, you're a girl. People expect boys to be sporty. Specially when you go to the sort of school I do.'

I looked at him, sympathetically. 'Don't you like school?' I said

'I hate it!'

'Don't you have any friends there?'

'I don't have any friends at all,' said Simon. 'Except for you.'

My heart went all melty when he said that. But I couldn't help thinking how sad it was, not to have friends.

'Maybe you could leave and come to our school,' I said.

He frowned. 'I don't think your mum and dad would want me living with them all week.'

'Why not?'

'Sam wouldn't like it.'

'Oh, well! *Sam*,' I said. 'She's just got the hump. She'll get over it.'

'What about Gus?'

'He'll just have to learn,' I said.

I couldn't help noticing, that evening, that the Radish seemed to be avoiding me. When we sat down to watch telly, he squeezed up next to Sam; and when Simon offered to play Snakes & Ladders with him, he just shook his head and thumb-sucked. I thought perhaps he was in a sulk 'cos of me being a bit snappish with him last night. I was sorry I'd been snappish, but he had got to *learn*. If Mum wasn't careful, he'd end up as a real spoilt brat.

8

All that week, the Radish avoided me. Well, not *avoided*, exactly; but it was Sam's hand that he held on the way home from school, and Sam he cuddled up to on the sofa. I tried to make it up with him.

I said, 'What about a game of Snakes & Ladders, then?'

He wouldn't even play Snakes & Ladders!

So then I said, 'Would you like to come and help me with my garden?'

He'd been badgering me, early on, to let him help with the garden. I'd said no, 'cos quite honestly the Radish is hopeless at anything like that. Cutting things, colouring things, making things. I knew he'd only mess it up. But now I was *offering*. I suppose I expected him to be grateful. Just a little bit. Well! He wasn't. He simply shook his head and said, 'No!' and rushed away. Which was when I gave up and decided to let him get on with it. If he wanted to sulk, that was up to him. I'd done what I could. You can pussyfoot too much, if you ask me.

I love that word, pussyfoot! It means creeping round on your tippity-toes, like a cat, so as not to upset someone. I decided that I was tired of pussyfooting round the Radish. I was going to start clumping, instead!

So I simply took no notice of him and got on doing my own thing. Simon had built me a frame for the front garden and I was busy making trees to go in it. The way I made them, I collected some interesting twigs from the garden, twigs with lots of spiky bits, then I cut long strips of leaves, all different shapes and sizes, from green crinkly paper – dark green, light green, yellowy green, cabbage green – and I twisted them round till they looked like they were growing.

Sam came into the shed to watch me. She said, 'Why don't you get twigs with real leaves on them?'

' 'Cos the leaves would die and fall off,' I said.

'Well, but that's what leaves *do*,' said Sam.

I didn't quite know what to say to that.

'You'll have a garden that's always summer!'

'I like summer.'

'Yeah, but it's not natural. They're supposed to die and then grow again. Unless they're evergreens, of course. Are yours evergreens?'

'Some might be.'

'What about the others? The ones that aren't evergreen?'

'What about them?' I said.

'They're supposed to die and then come back again!'

'But they wouldn't come back again, would they?' I said. ' 'Cos the twigs'd be dead.'

'That's all right! You could just go and get some more. Just pick them out the garden. Be a lot less hassle than all this.' She waved a hand at my scissors and crêpe paper.

'I like all this,' I said.

'Oh! Well. If you like it,' said Sam.

'I do! That's why I'm doing it.'

'So why didn't you just *say*? Honestly!' grumbled Sam. 'I was only trying to help!'

On Wednesday evening the telephone rang and it was Simon. Ringing to speak to *me*!

He said, 'How's the garden getting on?'

'It's nearly finished,' I said. And then I did my tomato act. I blushed bright scarlet. I have never heard of *anyone* blushing on the telephone. I mean, that is just pathetic.

'How's the Radish?'

'Hmmm . . .' I crinkled my nose. 'He's practically refusing to talk to me.'

'Why?' said Simon. 'What have you done?'

'I was mean to him. That night.'

'What, when he nearly shut Felix in the wahsing machine?'

'Yes. It's really worrying,' I said.

'I'm sure he didn't mean it.'

'I know, but it's still worrying. I keep wondering what he'll do next. Mum says he's insecure, but I don't see why he should take it out on the animals.'

'Maybe he'd be better off in a place without any animals. Maybe he's feeling a bit jealous of them.'

That had never occurred to me. I wondered if it could possibly be true. I didn't like to talk about it to Mum 'cos the last thing I wanted was to put ideas in her head and have her say the animals would have to go. I didn't *think* that she would, but you never can tell with grown-ups. The same went for Dad – which only left Sam.

Sam poured scorn on the idea.

'Course he isn't jealous of the animals! Stupid thing to say. He's just going through a bad patch. We all go through bad patches. Well, some of us do. Some of us that don't have proper homes and mums and dads like other people. You wouldn't know,' said Sam. 'You're privileged, you are.'

'I can't help it!' I said.

'No, and the Radish couldn't help that he was

bashed about and gets scared of things.'

'I never said he could!'

'You said he was jealous of the animals. That is just *crap*,' said Sam.

Crap's a word Mum doesn't like us using. But I didn't say anything 'cos Sam was quite worked up.

'If old Smarmypants hadn't come, none of this would ever have happened!'

I didn't want to quarrel with her. I went off to the shed and got on with my garden. I knew that Sam resented Simon. Some of the girls in our class, the ones who'd been at Lissie's party, or had heard about it, had started teasing me about having a boyfriend. I didn't mind, even though it made me blush. But Sam just huffed and made these scoffing noises.

'We don't do things together any more,' she complained, as we walked home on Friday afternoon. 'You're always stuck in the shed or up in your room, messing about with twigs and bits of paper.'

'I want to get it finished,' I said. And then, after a bit of a struggle, ' 'You could always come and help me.'

'I don't want to help you!'

I was kind of relieved when she said that. Sam's idea of helping is to take over and boss you around so that you end up having to do everything her way and getting all cross and irritated.

'I want us to do things.'

'Like what?'

'We could go up the park and play tennis.'

I'm hopeless at tennis.

'We could go swimming.'

I'm hopeless at swimming, too.

'We could go up the shopping centre, Sunday morning,' I said. 'I want to get some more crinkly paper.'

Sam groaned. And then she said, 'Oh, all right!'

'And then maybe we could go swimming *afterwards*,' I said. ''Cos I do like us doing things together and there has to be give and take in a relationship. (I know this. I read it in one of Mum's magazines that she has.)

'I suppose *he*'ll be there when we get back. He's not going swimming with us! Is he?' Sam made it sound almost threatening. 'If he's going to come, then I don't want to go!'

I sighed. There were times when I really wished Sam wasn't quite so extreme. Of course it's what makes her so bold and brave and funny. But it also makes her *diff-i-cult*.

'Well?' she said.

Her eyes bored into mine.

'Well, I . . . I think we'd have to ask him,' I pleaded. 'It'd only be polite.'

'In that case, I'm not going!'

'Maybe he won't want to,' I said, lamely.

But he did! I asked him after tea, when we were out in the shed looking at my garden, and he said that he would love to. So then I was faced with the prospect of having to tell Sam . . .

I decided that I would leave it for a bit. I

suppose it was rather cowardly of me, but I just didn't want us falling out right at the start of the weekend.

Saturday morning I went to my art class. I love going there! It is very quiet and peaceful and *dedicated*, everyone just wanting to draw and paint. Sam wouldn't have enjoyed it at all!

Dad took me there and picked me up again afterwards. He parked the car and we went into the house. Dad peeled off into the sitting room to watch sport on the telly, while I went down the hall to the kitchen.

Actually, I don't want to write this next bit. I hate even just thinking about it. Sometimes, even now, I have nightmares.

But I suppose I have to do it.

As I went into the kitchen I heard the sound of squealing. Animal squealing. The sort of squeal they do when you accidentally tread on their paws or shut the door on a tail. I tore across to the back door, but before I could reach it Jack had come bursting through. He was shaking his head – *flap flap flap!* – and blood was spurting everywhere. I think I must have screamed, and yelled for Mum, though I can't really remember. But anyway, next thing I know Mum's rushing through one door and Simon's rushing through the other. Mum comes from the house, Simon from the garden.

'What's the matter?' cries Mum. 'What's—' And then she sees Jack flapping his head and spurting blood, and she goes, 'Oh, my God! What's happened?'

Simon stammers, 'It was D-Daisy. She attacked him.'

'*Daisy?*' Now Sam's come racing in. She was in the sitting room, watching telly with Dad. 'Daisy never attacks anyone!'

'What's she done to him?' I screamed. 'What's she done to him?'

Me and Mum are trying to grab hold of Jack so we can see where he's been hurt, but he won't let us catch him. He lights out again, back into the garden, and the four of us go streaming after him.

Daisy's out there, lying on the grass munching a chew stick. And out of the corner of my eye I see the Radish, cringing into the shadows by the shed door. He's terrified of violence.

'I think she got his ear—' said Simon.

'His *ear*?'

Poor Jack's tearing round the garden, round and round in big circles, shaking his head and still spurting blood. And now Dad's out there, demanding to know what all the noise is about.

'It's Jack!' I screech. 'Daisy's bitten his ear!'

And then at last Mum manages to capture him, and we see that Jack's poor little ear hasn't just been bitten, it's been chewed right off. Well, the tip of it. He's only got half an ear! I immediately burst into loud sobs and have to be comforted by Dad.

'All right, all right,' says Mum. 'It's not the end of the world! I'm sure it looks far worse than it really is. Why don't you and Dad rush him down to the vet, just for a quick check, while I stay here and clean up the mess?'

'Yes, and I'll come with you,' says Simon.

So. We fetched a blanket for the seat and Simon and me sat in the back, with me holding Jack wrapped up in a towel and trying not to shed too many tears 'cos as Mum had said, it probably looked far worse than it really was. I mean, it wasn't like it was life-threatening, or anything. It had just spoilt his poor little darling ear!

'It was my fault,' said Simon. 'I shouldn't have given Daisy that chew stick.'

'You mean,' I hiccuped, 'you gave her one and not Jack?'

'I'm really sorry,' said Simon. 'I didn't think he'd notice. I was just . . .' He waved a hand. Jack instantly growled and curled his lip.

'He doesn't mean it,' I said, quickly. 'It's 'cos he's had a shock.'

'I think we've all had a shock,' said Dad. 'I thought someone had been murdered out there.'

'It was bad doggy psychology,' said Simon; and I remember, even at the time, being enormously impressed by the phrase. *Doggy psychology!*

'I was trying to get her to be friends with me. I mean, I'd like them both to be friends with me, but I thought I'd try with Daisy first.'

'Yes, 'cos she's so meek,' I said. Except that she hadn't been meek with Jack. She'd chewed off half his ear! My tears started flowing all over again.

'She just flew at him,' said Simon. 'He tried to get the chew stick off her and she just, like, went mad.'

'She's never done anything like that before,' I wept.

'Well, there's always a first time,' said Dad. 'Dogs will be dogs. And this is going to cost us a fortune, on a Saturday morning!'

The vet doesn't have a normal surgery on a Saturday. You have to make a special appointment or come in as an emergency. We were an emergency. I mean, we had to check that he didn't need stitches or anything.

Simon stayed in the waiting room while I

went in with Dad. The vet examined Jack carefully and told us that there wasn't any need for stitches, so that was a relief. But then he told us something else. He told us that Jack hadn't been bitten by Daisy, or any other dog.

'Somebody,' he said, 'did this with a pair of scissors.'

I told you I didn't want to write this bit. I just went cold all over when the vet said that. If I hadn't been holding Jack, with Dad right next to me, I think I might almost have fainted. I never *have* fainted. But I felt all shaky and shivery and the room sort of lurched. And then it passed and I just felt sick.

We went back to the car.

'What did he say?' said Simon.

I couldn't speak. It was Dad who told him.

'Oh.' Simon had suddenly turned very pale.

'Why did you say it was Daisy?' said Dad.

Simon swallowed. I could see his Adam's apple bob up and down.

'I didn't want you to know.'

'Know what?'

'That it was the Radish.'

'The Radish?' Dad half turned, in his seat. 'You're saying the *Radish* did it?'

Reluctantly, Simon nodded. And then I remembered . . . the Radish, crouched by the shed door with something in his hand. Something glinting and gleaming . . . a pair of scissors! Dad's big scissors out of the shed.

Simon explained how he had been in the shed, with the Radish just pottering about. Suddenly he had heard Jack squeal, and had rushed out to find the Radish with the scissors and Jack hurtling up the garden, spurting blood.

'You should have told us,' said Dad.

'I'm sorry.' Simon lowered his gaze. 'I didn't want to get him into trouble.'

'I can see that,' said Dad. 'But this is serious.'

I didn't say anything. My brain was kind of exploding. All I could think was 'Jack – the Radish. Jack – the Radish,' over and over like an old gramophone record that's got stuck.

When we got back, Mum and Sam were still sponging down the kitchen. Blobs of blood were splattered everywhere. I never knew an ear could bleed so much. Dad told them what the vet had said. Mum's eyes opened wide.

'So who—'

'Gus.'

'*Gus?*'

'I knew it wasn't Daisy!' cried Sam.

'Where is Gus?' said Dad.

Mum and Sam had been so busy with the kitchen they'd clean forgotten about the Radish. We went into the garden and there he was, just as we had left him, crouched by the shed. The scissors were still in his hand.

'How could he do it?' I sobbed.

'He couldn't!' It was Sam who shouted it. 'How could the Radish have done it? You know what he's like! He can't cut anything! And anyway' – she spun round, accusingly – 'he's left-handed!'

It was true. The Radish *is* left-handed – and the scissors were in his right hand. It is also true that he suffers from very poor co-ordination. It was the reason I hadn't let him help me with my garden. The Radish is so unco-ordinated he can hardly tie his shoelaces, let alone handle a pair of scissors. It's something to do with the way he was treated by his mum's boyfriend.

I took a deep, quivering breath. If the Radish hadn't done it . . .

'Let me talk to him,' said Mum. 'The rest of you:' She made shooing motions at us.

'He probably won't be able to remember anything,' said Simon.

Sam looked at him very hard.

'We'll see,' said Mum.

I don't know where Sam and Dad went. Back to the telly, probably. I went upstairs with Jack. We lay on my bed and cuddled, and I wept all over again. I wept partly because of his poor ear and partly because of the sudden horror that had descended on us. Sam had said I was privileged, and I knew now that she was right. Before now, nothing really bad had ever happened to me.

I must have cried myself to sleep because next thing I remember was opening my eyes to find that the hands of the clock had whizzed on by nearly two hours. It was sounds from somewhere downstairs that had woken me. I crept out on to the landing and peered over the banisters. I was just in time to see Simon going through the front door with a lady I recognised as Social Services. She was the one who'd brought dear old Ellen to us in the middle of the night when Ellen's mum had been taken to hospital.

I immediately raced across the landing into Mum and Dad's room, to look out of the window. I saw the Social Services lady take out her car keys, open the door of her car and stand back to let Simon into the front seat. Just before she shut the door on him, he turned and glanced up. I don't think he saw me. I hope he didn't. I wouldn't have wanted to be seen by him.

'Abi?' Mum was coming up the stairs.

'I was just looking out the w-w—'

'I know, I know.' Mum put her arm round

me. 'Come and sit down. We have to talk.'

I suppose Mum didn't tell me anything I hadn't already worked out. It had been Simon all along. *He'd* told the Radish to shoot an arrow at Felix. *He'd* told him to chop up the worms. He'd been the one to try and shut Felix in the washing machine. He'd been the one to cut off Jack's ear – and then put the scissors into the Radish's hand and told him to 'stay there'.

'But why didn't the Radish tell us?' I wept.

'He couldn't, Abi. He was too scared. Simon had threatened to – do things to him.'

'Oh, Mum!' I just hurled myself into her arms and cried and cried. I couldn't understand what would make anyone be so cruel. Mum said she couldn't either. She said, 'We don't always have answers for these things, Abi. Nobody does. But Simon's very angry, he's very hurt. He feels life has let him down – and so he's taking his revenge. He's just hitting out every way he can. He needs a lot of help, but we're not the people to give it to him.'

'I hate him!' I wept. 'I hate him for what he did!'

'Try not to,' urged Mum. 'I know it's difficult, but . . . he wasn't all bad. Nobody is all bad.'

I thought of the way he'd helped me with my garden, and I knew that what Mum said was true: there *was* a good side to him. A gentle, caring side. But just at that moment I felt I would never be able to forgive him. I told Mum, and she said, 'You will, one day. I promise you.'

Mum is usually right. I shall just have to wait and see.

'Stay here for a few minutes,' said Mum. 'Sam wants to talk to you.'

I wasn't sure that I wanted Sam talking to me, I was certain she would gloat and say I told you so. I heard her bounding up the stairs – she always takes them three at a time – and then her head appeared round the door and she said, 'Can I come in?' and came in anyway.

'He's gone,' she said.

'Yes,' I said. 'I know.'

'Has Mum told you everything?'

'Yes.'

'Abi, I'm really sorry!'

' 's all right,' I said. I scrubbed at my eyes. 'How's the Radish?'

'Much happier now it's all out. We've been playing Snakes & Ladders! I promised him you'd play with him later.' Then she paused and said, 'I *am* sorry, Ab. Honestly! 'Cos I know you liked him.'

'I was just stupid,' I mumbled.

'No, you weren't! Everybody thought he was gorgeous. Even Lissie and Mary-Jo.'

'You didn't,' I said.

'N-no. But I bet I would have done, if he hadn't been so snooty. I bet then,' said Sam, 'I'd have had a thing about him, too! And then we'd have quarrelled.'

'We don't quarrel,' I said, fiercely.

'No, we don't.' Sam bounced herself on to my bed. 'Coming swimming tomorrow, then? Just the two of us?'

I nodded, gratefully.

'It'll be nice,' said Sam, 'just you and me together. Like it used to be. After all –' she pulled one of her faces – 'boys! Who needs 'em?'

I suddenly felt happier.

'Boys!' I cried. 'Who needs them?'

And then I thought, well, except for the Radish . . . I sprung off the bed. Sam sprang after me.

'Where are you going?'

'Going to find the Radish,' I said.

I was going to give him the hugest big hug of all time!